AF613214

ISBN-13 (Paperback): 979-8-9863022-1-8

ISBN-13 (Kindle): 979-8-9863022-0-1

Edited by: Wendy Muruli

Cover design by: Chloe Arzuaga

The Ghosts of Poplar Valley

Besu Tadesse

Prologue

May 16, 1987, 1:44 AM

Aida looked up and saw her friend's lifeless corpse – bloody knuckles, fists tied with twine, pants down, eyes open and staring into the void. In the light flickering of the lantern, a greenish glow dancing on the ground, she saw the noose tightly wound around her friend's neck, tongue sticking out to one side with the fresh stench of death filling her nose. Aida began to experience tunnel vision, her mind and ears washing away hysterical screaming while her eyes focused on burn marks across the thighs and dismembered genitals. Her heart started beating harder and faster, the silence in her mind replaced with a blistering high-pitched ringing, slowly shifting from a nuisance in her ears to a pounding feeling in her head. She was disoriented and unable to move her body. The ringing became louder, the pain in her head greater, and her heartbeat fast enough to the point of dizziness and collapse, until a hand on her shoulder pulled her back to reality.

Chapter 1

May 15, 1987, 5:15 PM

"Can we please not do this?" Aida was tired of her friends getting into long-winded, needless arguments. The van continued down the road, kicking up dry, reddish Georgia dust in the air.

"I can't help that he's being so sensitive," Luke sneered. He turned back to Marcus. "You have to stop making excuses for people. Those people make their choices every day."

"Shut up. You have no idea what you're talking about." Marcus was generally good-natured and easy going, but he never took kindly to Luke dismissing him. "You haven't even opened up a history book, have you?"

On this day, the argument started as it usually did, with a politically charged statement about oppression in the United States and Luke challenging him loudly with a large amount of condescension in his voice. The argument today was especially lively because of the energy that came from graduating high school, as well as the desire to show off a bit of their intellect in front of their friends before they leave for college and start the rest of their lives. Regardless, the conversation was entirely too intense for a weekend vacation.

"So you're saying that successful people didn't earn their places in society, and the lazy and undeserving people should just have everything?" Luke spoke with sharpness in his voice and added extra emphasis on the word *lazy*.

"What I'm saying is that people who look like you haven't been earning their places since the beginning of this country. This country gave you a head start. And we're not going to get any better if we don't give people a chance!" Marcus was filled with righteous indignation.

"So because I'm white, I didn't earn my place?"

"Now you're twisting my words."

"What he's saying," BG interjected from the passenger seat of the van, "is that we've been getting some chances that others haven't been able to get, so the only way that we can begin to fix it is to set aside some space for others to get a chance."

"Well, not the only way, but one of the ways," agreed Marcus.

"But I don't understand how being racist towards white people is going to help," sniped Luke.

Marcus took a couple of breaths to calm down, then he gave a quick smirk. He wouldn't be baited. "At this point,

I think you're just doing this to mess with me. You can't be this dumb."

"Don't be mad because you don't have any argument."

"Can everyone just stay quiet for two seconds?" Aida, until now, had tried to ignore their incessant arguing. She relaxed her body, enjoying oscillating periods of silent contemplation and feisty conversation. But after listening to fifteen minutes of an increasingly obnoxious debate Aida was losing her patience.

"Don't tell me that you agree with him." Marcus was pleading for support.

"I really just want to enjoy the drive without hearing you two yell at each other all the way to the lake."

"But you *do* agree." He turned to Luke. "See, Luke, looks like you're the only one that believes this nonsense."

Luke snapped back, "Yeah, the only one in *this* car. Most people in the town agree with me. Most people in the country probably agree with me."

"About half of the people in this country *might* agree with you, and they're wrong."

"How can half of the people be wrong?"

"Because half of the people probably failed basic history."

Edmond interjected from the back seat of the van, sitting next to Marcus. "Seriously, guys, please stop." Edmond was even less interested than Aida in hearing this. Edmond dealt with his own issues as a child of Japanese immigrants and could not be bothered. "You guys do this almost every time we meet up, and it's just a waste of time. Plus, you're triggering my anxiety."

Luke casually chided him. "First of all, I'm having fun taking him down. Second, I don't understand why Marcus acts like he's oppressed all the time." Again, Luke put a longer, more condescending attitude on the word *oppressed*.

Marcus was agitated. "Listen, I know you get to be part of the big family in Lorro, but my family has spent most of the time in this country being oppressed. My ancestors were slaves, and their children had to deal with segregation, Jim Crow, and all these other problems. My family used to live around here and they had to leave, and my family somehow found their way back. Getting to move into the nice part of town? That happened just two years ago. I know you can't figure out why some people might be a little upset that they have to do so much more."

Luke became more irritated. "Stop acting like you can't get ahead. You're near the top of the class, and…"

Marcus interrupted with a smug look: "*At* the top of the class, thank you."

Luke rolled his eyes. "... *at* the top of the class, and you act like you don't have the same chances that I do. Our dads have the same great jobs. We go to the same school and live in the same gated part of the same neighborhood." The rest of their friends winced at his smarmy comment about living in the "gated part". "And if you hate this country so much, why are you going to West Point? To the military, for the United States? It doesn't make sense."

"First of all, I plan to use the training to build something else beyond this country's history. Second, we only have *one* high school, so everyone goes there. Third, you can *still* get ahead without having to work so hard. You don't even have good grades, but you got into the same colleges that I did. Don't blame me because you're dumb."

"I'm not dumb!"

Edmond's anxiety had been increasing with each minute of the never-ending tirade. He blurted out, "For God's sake, you're both dumb. Now please shut up!"

Marcus's face relaxed, and he settled back into his seat. Luke's face did not budge, but he did lean back into this seat as well. Luke sighed and whispered to himself, "I'm not dumb..."

After a brief and awkward silence, Lisa, who has been quietly driving the van during all of this, spoke up.

"Hey Aida, what are you doing next year?"

"I'm planning to stay in state."

BG looked over his shoulder and chimed into the conversation. "Hey, me too!"

Aida's face lit up. "Oh, nice. I did alright in class, so I figured I'd stay in state at least two years to save some money." She tilted her head toward Marcus and Luke. "I don't really have the money like *these* guys over here."

Marcus smirked a little. Luke was silent and continued staring out of the van window.

"Lisa, what do you plan to do?"

"I'm going out of state." Lisa was dodgy.

"Any idea specifically?"

"Somewhere that will pay me to run."

"Luke, you still going to the Ivy League?" Marcus emphasized the words *Ivy League*. Luke was pouting and did not want to answer. "Come on, man." Luke stayed silent.

Marcus continued. "Whatever, man. I'm going to West Point. I'm not sure if I fully want to commit to the army, but I figure it could open some doors for me in the future. Maybe even politics. Edmond, what are you doing next year?"

"I think I'm going to stick around Lorro for a bit, probably work at my parents' shop. Get my head straight. Maybe go see my family in Japan for a little while before I come back to help '*grow the family's empire*'." He said the last part with contempt.

As they continued talking about their future plans, Luke looked down and noticed a comic book in between the driver's and passenger's seats.

"What's that?"

BG replied, "What's what?"

"That thing next to your foot. Is that a comic book?"

BG glanced down quickly to check, then moved his eyes forward to look out the windshield. He was visibly annoyed for the ignorant "nerd" statements that were going to come from Luke.

"Yeah."

"Why did you bring that *nerd* stuff on the trip?"

BG rolled his eyes and audibly sighed. "Whatever, man."

"No, seriously, tell me about it. I want to know."

Marcus intervened. "BG, you really don't have to talk about it."

BG insisted, "No, no. If he wants to learn about it, I'll tell him about it."

Luke sneered., "Oh, I do." Against his better judgment, BG decided to tell him. He sighed, turned his body over the passenger's seat to make eye contact with Luke, then proceeded with the story.

"Alright. There's this girl that's part of an intergalactic police force, and she flies around with a magic ring that lets her do anything. She fights this invincible zombie with large arms that has been infused with swamp stuff and can't die, who has been causing problems for a long time. But she actually saves him from a glacier, and ever since then, he decides to protect her and help her. It gets more complicated throughout the story, but it's pretty interesting when..."

Toward the end of his explanation, Luke rolled his eyes and simulated a loud, drawn-out snoring sound. BG sighed and stopped talking. He knew how Luke mocked him. Lisa reached her hand out to hold BG's hand and help him calm down.

Lisa turned her head over her right shoulder to address Luke. "You're a dick." Luke was taken aback, as was the rest of the car. Even BG flinched a bit. He was not used to hearing Lisa speak so forwardly and aggressively. "You've been bothering us this whole time. Just because we're using your family's car doesn't mean you get to talk to us however you feel like it."

Luke was still stunned, and he hesitated to speak until he knew what to say. "Geez, Lisa, I'm sorry. I didn't realize you felt that way. I thought your people would be calmer, like Eddie back here."

Lisa was confused.

"Shut up." Edmond was more than confused. He became visibly annoyed. "And if you're going to talk about me, use my full name. Don't disrespect me."

Aida saw that Edmond was ready to lose his temper and turned to him. She mouthed the words "Please don't" before he could say or do anything reckless. The kids were planning to spend the rest of the weekend together and having known Edmond for several years and been witness to his anxious tirades, she knew that this could sour the entire trip. She also knew that Luke had made two crucial errors. First, Edmond never liked the nickname "Eddie." He did not want any colorful nicknames. Even his parents called him Edmond and nothing else. Lisa was about to highlight his second mistake.

"Why would you bring up Edmond? We're not the same person."

Luke was oblivious to what he was saying. Yeah, but you're from the same country, right?"

Lisa tried to keep calm, but she was close to losing her cool. She quickly turned back to face the road. Now BG reached his hand to her shoulder to calm her down, returning the favor from earlier. Aida looked at Edmond to make sure that he was alright. By this time, he had closed his eyes and tried to relax. Aida slowly spoke."Look, we've been through this. Lisa was born here and her family is Korean. Edmond and his family are from Japan. I'm assuming you know the difference."

Luke showed his ignorance. "Yes, of course I know the difference, Aida. It's just that no one told me that *they* were different." He emphasized *they* while nodding and pointing to Lisa and Edmond. "And, I'll be honest, I can't tell."

"You can't be serious. Please say fewer words."

By this point, no one but Aida wanted to make eye contact with Luke, let alone speak with him. Luke was tired of being singled out, and he lashed back. "Of *course* I'm serious. There aren't a lot of Asians around our little town, you know. Can you tell the difference between all of the Irish people that live in the town?"

Aida was confused. "I mean, not really, but is there really anyone directly *from* Ireland in our town anymore."

"See that? You can't figure it out. But that's not really important. The point is that I didn't know something, and now I do. Maybe I should have known before I got into the car, but I didn't. Hell, Aida, you've got tan skin and curly hair, but if I didn't know any better, you and Marcus could be related. You could *at least* be cousins."

She mocked Luke. "Yes, Luke, I'm related to Marcus, and we have all of the same aunts and uncles from Italy."

"Look, all I'm saying is look at you. It's summer, you've got tan skin and dark, curly hair. And your sisters look like me. You look like Martin Luther King next to the rest of your family!"

Aida did have a tan glow in contrast to her three sisters, who all had paler skin. There were pictures of her family throughout her house, pictures where people would come to the house and ask about who that "other" girl was. By contrast, Marcus and his family, the Dixons, were one of the few Black families in the entire town of Lorro. Both Marcus and his father were lighter skinned than Marcus's mother, whose skin resembled a smooth chocolate bar. One with less discerning senses, such as Luke, could confuse Marcus and Aida as kin.

Aida joined the rest of the group, turning her entire body away from Luke and staring out the van into the ever-moving landscape. Marcus had found his Discman portable CD player and headphones and zoned out of any conversation. Realizing he was defeated, Luke grabbed the comic book from the front, pretending to be interested, and stayed quiet, doing his best to not make his friends angry again.

Chapter 2

May 15, 5:27 PM

Luke broke the lengthy, awkward silence.

"Hey Eddie, can you pass me a bag of potato chips?" he asked, turning backwards to Edmond. Luke did not seem to remember anything. Everyone knew that Luke was never keen on apologizing for anything, either.. Edmond, having been on the receiving end of Luke's annoying comments more than anyone else over the years, developed a cold indifference to him. Edmond rolled his eyes as he checked the gap between where he was sitting at the back of the van and the tailgate. He responded with an emotionless, cold, "whatever."

As Edmond reached back over his left shoulder, his hands fiddled around while a confused look came over his face. He did not feel the bag. He leaned back to find them.

"I don't see them."

"Well, where did you put them?" asked Luke. Luke's tone of arrogance would not be welcome, except Edmond was responsible for securing the snacks for the trip.

"I don't remember, but they should be around. Did anyone else take them?"

Marcus pulled his headphones away from his ears and set his CD player aside as he saw Edmond's commotion. "What's going on?"

"I can't find the snacks," Edmond blurted as he shuffled through the back of the car.

"You didn't put them in the car?"

"That was BG's job."

"No it wasn't," BG casually stated from the front of the car. "I gave you those snacks to load while I went home to get my extra sleeping bag."

Luke was irritated. "Dude, we paid a lot of money to get those snacks for the trip. Don't tell me you guys forgot to put them in the car."

Marcus interjected. "Yeah man, we need prepared food. They didn't rebuild the fire pits since that whole thing a few years ago, and I don't want to eat uncooked cold cuts."

"Don't worry, I brought a hot plate," Lisa reassured.

Everyone in the car looked at each other, then along the floor of the car and in between seats, looking for any trace of the large plastic bag that held their treats.

Marcus ran his hands under his seat. "Nothing under here."

Aida casually glanced down and feigned searching. "I don't see anything down here either." She was committed to enjoying the road scenery without any more interruption.

"Do you guys have anything up there?" Luke asked sharply to Lisa.

"No," Lisa was short, still upset about the exchange from earlier. She made it obvious that she was not looking for the bag.

"Seriously, I'm sorry for pissing you off, but can you please check?"

She looked quickly between the front seats. "They're not up here."

Luke sighed an exasperated sigh. "BG, did you leave them at home?"

BG blurted in a matter-of-fact tone, "Like I said, I wasn't responsible for them."

"Are you stupid or something?"

BG yelled out without thinking, "Pull over!" Everyone in the car froze, except for Lisa who kept calm behind the wheel.

The car suddenly pulled sharply to the right into the shoulder lane, which jerked everyone into the left of the car. The tires ran over coarse, rocky ground. Dust billowed into the air and puffed around the back of the van as it came to an abrupt stop.

"What did you say?" He spoke in an eerily calm tone that was known to unnerve those that made him angry. His usually calm demeanor quickly melted away. Luke had been getting on his nerves since they set foot in the car. BG turned his head over his left shoulder, flexing muscles that were better suited for an offensive lineman despite never having played any sport.

Luke stammered. "Um…"

BG, still and calm while he leaned his upper body toward Luke and puffed his chest out: "No, go on. Say what you just said again."

Luke did not want to put his well-being in danger. He spoke with a mild tremble in his voice. "Look, I'm just a bit hungry. I just get a little upset when I haven't eaten, you know that."

BG was satisfied that he had put enough fear into him and relaxed his body. "Well, if you need something, we can just stop off somewhere on the way. Is that alright with you?

Luke spoke tentatively. "Yeah, man, of course."

BG then turned to everyone else in the van. "Everyone else

okay with that?" Marcus flashed a smile and a thumbs up. Edmond nodded. Aida smiled back at him to acknowledge the question. She had known BG long enough to know he would not lose his temper, and she was a little amused by his silencing of Luke.

BG's voice calmed. "Good." Lisa shifted the van back into the "drive" position and slowly pulled back onto the road.

Suddenly from the back of the van, Edmond blurted out, "Oh wait! I think I found them!" He quickly pulled a dull yellow bag from deep underneath the seat. Everyone became excited that they were not going to go hungry. Then Edmond's face fell as he opened the bag. "No, wait, sorry everyone. It's my laundry."

Luke screamed as he clasped his hands on his forehead. "Are you serious?!" The friends were starting to get hungry, so no one chastised him for the outburst.

Marcus's excitement turned to confusion. "How did your laundry end up in the van?"

"I'm so sorry. I took the wrong one. I think they bags were the same color." The rest of them slid a little further down in the seats.

Disappointed, BG asked, "Does anyone know where we can stop off to get some more food?"

Aida chimed in. "I don't think so. I've been to the lake a

lot, and I don't remember any stores being on or off the road."

Marcus agreed. "Yeah, me neither."

"I don't know, either, babe, but I'm sure we can find something." Lisa had a slight smile on her face while she spoke. She always loved BG, no matter what he was doing, but she loved him a little more when he took authority.

"Well, don't worry about it. There's a store right there." BG nodded forward, slightly to his right.

Lisa was puzzled. "Where?"

"That one right there. Next to that big tree."

In the distance was a general store attached to a small bed and breakfast. The store had a small table with two wooden chairs, and the store served as the breakfast side of the operation. Beside the store was a large tree with a large white trunk and wrinkly bark, adorned with thick branches and a lush green color. Throughout the tree, there were small, white, fluffy seeds strewn about the leaves, as if the tree had been dusted with cotton balls. As they approached along the road, a small hand-painted sign appeared on the road announcing the name: The Cottonwood Inn.

Aida looked over. "Oh, good. Let's stop there."

Lisa pulled the van into the dusty patch that made up the driveway, where they saw the Cottonwood Inn more clearly. The white wood of the facade was rotted with large brown cracks across its planks, aged by the beating of Georgia weather and the passing of time. The roof tiles were worn and dangling, an indication that the inn's best days were long past. A tree with a straw hat and smiling face was drawn next to the door, presenting the tree as a folksy doorman welcoming you to the store with one of its green, rounded limbs. A small porch with two stairs led to a rickety door with a small square peephole carved out to see entering customers and scare away any trouble.

A small, empty, child-sized rocking chair sat next to the entrance door, rocking slowly and steadily. An outdoor woodworking area was behind the store, visible past the left side of the building. The most notable part of the inn was the large, imposing cottonwood tree, the first thing that the friends saw when they pulled onto the lot. Located about fifty feet from the building's façade, the tree boasted a height over one hundred feet, and the soil beneath the tree had a reddish clay hue. When looking past the large cottonwood tree from the inn's entrance, the change from the light brown dustiness of the red clay dust to the darker browns and greens in the background forest gave the scene a haunting view. The wrinkles in the bark gave the appearance of a group of people tussling with each other while a behemoth towered above them, watching their every move.

There was not a lot of space to pull the van in once they drove past the driveway. Lisa looked over the hood and was not convinced she could fit the van safely.

"There isn't much space to even park. Probably enough space for two cars, but not a lot of space to back out when we want to leave. Do we really need to stop here? We can just keep going."

"I'm already getting really hungry," whined Luke.

"Me too," BG agreed.

"I think I'll be okay." Marcus was unfazed.

"Me too," Aida agreed.

"I could eat a little," Edmond uttered from the back anxiously.

BG calmly took control as Lisa parked the van. "What does everyone want?"

"Can you get me some peanut butter pieces?" Lisa loved peanut butter. "If they don't have them, some peanut butter cups are fine."

Luke was enthusiastic. "And some potato chips."

"I'm okay", Marcus reiterated, still unfazed.

"Me too", Aida repeated from before.

Edmond was energetic and excited. "I'll get some popcorn. If not, some chips. Oh, and some cheesy puffs."

BG was annoyed at his friends' numerous requests, but he listened intently. "Alright, I think I got it. Be back in a second." BG opened his door and stepped out, the sound of his boots shuffling over rocks and dust.

"You don't want anything?" Lisa asked Marcus, curious.

"No, I'll just eat some sandwiches later."

Luke perked up. "Wait, you have sandwiches?"

"Yeah."

"Can I get one?'

Marcus dismissively replied, "No."

"Come on, man, I'm hungry."

Marcus did not bother to look at Luke. "You should find some food then."

"Man, I thought we were all going to just have the snacks."

Aida chimed in. "I brought some real food."

Edmond followed. "Yeah, me too. I thought we were just getting some community snacks. You thought we were just going to eat junk food all weekend?"

Luke was confused. "Well, yeah, I figured that was part of the fun."

Edmond smugly replied, "Are you stupid or something?"

Luke went back to being silent.

BG came back to the van empty-handed. "They're not open."

"Well, that's too bad," Lisa blurted out, trying to hide her enthusiasm. "We'll probably find something later."

"No, no, no, no, no. I need something to eat," Luke reiterated forcefully, getting more irritated that no one wanted to share food with him.

"Listen, the door is locked, and there is no light on. You want to just break in and take food?" asked BG, trying to understand what the fuss was about.

"Now that you mention it…" Luke's words stumbled out as he climbed over Aida to get out of the van.

"Hey! Get off me!" shouted Aida.

"Yeah, sorry about that." Luke rushed out to get food from the store. He quickly slid the door of his minivan so fast that Aida's fingers were almost caught in the sliding mechanism. Thankfully, Aida moved her hands quickly, avoiding a visit to the hospital in lieu of her vacation at the lake.

Luke began to walk up to the door of the inn but stopped short when he saw a little girl that was no more than eight years old, sitting in the rocking chair on the porch. She had bright brown eyes and wore a powder blue dress, kinky hair split down the middle into two pigtail puffs and each tied with a small orange ribbon. She wore tiny black boots, each with simple, bronze-colored clasps. Despite her bright eyes and adorable frame, she shot Luke two sharp eyes, a deliberate and unwelcoming glance that let Luke know that she was not interested in seeing him. Luke noticed and called out, trying to charm her.

"Hey, is your store open?" He exaggerated his voice and moved his head back and forth, doing his best impression of a charming person.

The girl was silent. She maintained her stare.

The façade quickly dissolved. Luke felt unnerved but would not give up. He continued through shaky nerves. "Is… is your family around?"

Still, the girl remained silent. Her eyes looked through Luke with an even deeper stare.

Luke felt uneasy and impatient. He was used to being told "no" over the years, especially when it came to dating. However, he did not like silence when he asked a basic question. His only instinct was to keep moving toward the store. He stopped after two steps.

"You better not come closer!" yelled the little girl, with the fire of a hundred suns burning in her eyes. Luke froze. He was stunned to see such a young girl talk to him that way. In an attempt to ease the tension and not wanting to feel embarrassed, Luke took a step back, turned around, and started walking back to the van.

Inside the van, his friends were restless and hoped to get back on the road and start their two-day respite before going home to prepare for their high school graduation. Luke returned to the sliding door of the van, defeated and weary from the encounter with the girl.

"I can't go in there."

"Why not?" asked Aida, sounding annoyed and contemptuous.

"I don't know, but something doesn't feel right. That little girl is freaking me out."

BG turned his head to Luke, his face scrunched. "Girl? What girl?"

"The one that's sitting on the rocking chair near the door. She's just weird."

The group looked out of their respective windows to see the little girl sitting on the chair and watching them from the rocking chair.

"That girl wasn't sitting there when I went to the door," BG uttered, confounded as to where the young girl came from and how she made her way to the rocking chair.

Marcus, never deterred from a challenge, brushed off their concerns. "She doesn't seem that bad. Damn, Luke, I know you get uncomfortable around Black people, but little Black girls too?" He gave a hint of sarcasm and derision knowing that it would get under Luke's skin. It worked.

"Oh, here we go again. It's always got to be about someone being Black," lamented Luke.

"Oh, relax, baby bear. Didn't mean anything by it."

"Stop it." Aida did not want another unnecessary conversation. "Can someone just grab the snacks?"

Luke was exasperated. "Yeah, I'd like to get to the camp before dark."

"She's making me feel anxious too," Edmond chimed from the back seat of the van.

"Man, you get anxious about everything. You've been anxious since Susie Davis made fun of you for spilling all that glitter on yourself when we were kids."

"That's not the point. *This* little girl is creeping me out."

"Me too," Lisa interjected, "but she's adorable, and she's probably nice if you just talk to her."

"Adorable?" asked Luke, with amazement.

"Yeah, I think I'll do that," declared Marcus, as he made his way politely over Edmond and out of the van. "Excuse me, Eddie."

The word "Eddie" slipped out of Marcus's mouth with the same sarcasm that he used to poke fun at Luke, but his charm and quick nod to Edmond let him know that he was joking with him. Marcus had a way with people, especially with saying something that any jerk would say, but without ever being perceived as one. In other words, he had the opposite effect of Luke. Marcus turned to Aida after he stepped out of the van and slightly past Luke. "Aida, you don't seem bothered by a little girl. You want to come?"

"Sure." She casually shrugged her shoulders and exited the car behind Marcus.

Marcus and Aida walked to the inn, where the same girl sat quietly in her chair. As they approached, she stared straight at Marcus, a smile appearing slowly across her face. Marcus noticed, and he made sure that Aida noticed.

"I keep telling you, people love me." Marcus swaggered in his blue-and-white rugby shirt, red shorts, and white sneakers.

Aida did her best to hold back a smirk, trying to bring his ego down. "Stop being weird. She's just a silly kid."

"You heard Luke. She didn't even try to talk to him. I can't help who I am." Notwithstanding his general arrogance, Marcus looked like he stepped out of the pages of a clothing catalog. Against Aida and her baggy sweatshirts and jogging pants, his style and demeanor were all the more striking.

They approached the girl calmly and smoothly.

"Hey, how are you?" Marcus asked the girl.

"I'm doing fine, sir." Her eyes widened and brightened, as if talking to an old friend or family member that she had not seen in years. Marcus shot Aida a glance, reinforcing his charm. He reflected her politeness.

"Is it alright if I go in to buy a few things, ma'am?"

The little girl was tickled at being called ma'am by someone clearly older than her. She played coy.

"Um… alright." She clasped her hands together and swung back and forth with a dimpled smile.

Aida chimed in. "Can I go in too, ma'am?"

The little girl quickly turned her head and scowled at Aida, who thought she could be just as charming. However, not long after scowling, the little girl's face changed from mean to puzzled. She leaned forward in her chair, looking deeper into Aida's face from afar, as if Aida were a foreign invader. She hopped out of her rocking chair and walked over to her, beckoning Aida to bend her face down to her level. Aida obliged, bending one knee to the ground.

The girl stared into Aida's eyes, searching for something that she didn't quite know she was looking for. She grabbed Aida's cheeks, pulling, and pushing, moving her head around and tussling the loose curly, dark brown locks of hair hanging off her ponytail. Aida became more confused and her face more contorted. Marcus laughed to himself.

"You're very pretty." The girl released her hands abruptly from Aida's face. "I'm sorry, I didn't realize. Of course, you can come in, too." Aida felt proud to have gotten the girl's approval. She had gained the trust that Luke could not. Aida stood up from her kneeling position, put her arms on her waist in a sassy fashion. "Well, good then." She took a step toward the door of the inn but stopped briefly. "Oh, by the way, what's your name young lady?"

"Dorothy. But my friends call me Dottie." The little girl was polite and confident.

"Nice to meet you, Dorothy."

"I said that my *friends* call me Dottie."

Aida gave a sassy smile. "So, we're friends now?"

"Yes, ma'am." Aida found it charming – *ma'am*.

"Does that mean we're friends, too?" asked Marcus, who had felt a bit pushed out of the conversation thus far.

Dorothy gave a flirty look. "Of course, *you* get to be my friend!"

Marcus feigned relief. "Whew, okay, good. I was a little concerned."

"Can our friends come in and become your fr---?" asked Aida.

Dorothy screamed abruptly, cutting off Aida. "No! They can't come in!"

Aida and Marcus were taken aback. They looked at each other with a short glance, trying to understand how Dottie could have changed her demeanor so quickly. Aida would not be swayed.

"Hey, Dottie. It's okay, they're with us. We'll make sure they don't do anything bad in the store."

Dottie thought for nearly ten seconds as she looked up at Aida. "Are you sure?"

"We promise. We'll make sure everything, and everyone, is okay."

Dorothy thought for another ten seconds. Aida and

Marcus were looking around, trying not to make too much eye contact with her or each other, waiting for this pint-sized gatekeeper to render her decision. Finally, she decided.

Dottie spoke with trepidation. "Okay. They can come too," Dorothy then gestured Aida and Marcus closer to her to whisper to them. "But you need to watch them. We don't *trust* them."

The group had been hungry on the road for too long and were not in the mood for endless negotiations with a child. They wanted to get their food and go as quickly as possible.

"Don't worry," Aida reassured her.

"Hmm… okay…" Dorothy stated this with little enthusiasm or reassurance. She gestured Aida and Marcus to follow her. After that, Aida and Marcus waved their friends over to the store. Seeing Marcus and Aida wave them over, Edmond, BG, and Luke decided that they would follow. Edmond jumped out of the car first, pushing past Luke on the way out and rushing to find a bathroom and some snacks.

He ran so fast that he slid past Marcus and just behind Aida while she walked into the store. Marcus glared at Edmond as he skirted past him. BG opened his door calmly to get food and drinks for himself and Lisa.

"You want to come babe?" he asked.

"No thanks. I'll just wait in the car. Just grab me some chips or something."

"No problem. See you in a couple of minutes."

BG stepped out and started heading to the store. Luke was hungry too, and he was not interested in staying in the car with someone that hated him. Lisa really hated him. He finally made it to the store just after BG entered.

Chapter 3

May 15, 5:38 PM

The Cottonwood Inn was not a pleasant sight. Inside the store were five short, stocky shelves that held cooking supplies and two moderately sized tables for pre-made baked goods. The baked goods looked and smelled unexpectedly appetizing in contrast to the drab interior of the store. There was a large bookshelf full of cracked, rotted wood near the back of the store, directly across from the entrance. There were very few books for the sale - a bible and some cookbooks - as well several yellow-tinged newspapers from unknown publications. The newspapers had a layer of dust that made it difficult to read headlines or articles, but the shelves were marked with two makeshift signs. The left sign read "Papers" and the right sign read "Announcements", with the pile of announcements stacking about three times the height of the newspapers.

To the left of the bookshelves was a doorway to the backyard and outhouse. To the left of that doorway was another opening for a separate hallway. The hallway led to two separate bedrooms, one with two small cots and another room with one solitary cot. The faint sound of construction could be heard from a distance.

The group looked around and tried to take in the earthy, decrepit decor. Even Marcus, normally the one with the most tact, winced a little as he ran his index finger across the dusty wall. Luke, known for being the least tactful, displayed a fully disgusted face and let out a deep, obvious guttural sound.

"Ugh," blurted Luke, audible enough for the shopkeeper to hear. Marcus whispered to Luke, "For once I agree with you." The group started to spread about the store, looking for refreshments.

BG took a softer approach. "Yeah, this place looks a little rough, but I'm sure we can find something." He glanced over the table of sweets and found a delicious treat. "That looks like a bear claw." He looked around and found a slender, shiny-faced woman sweeping the floor near the main counter. She was wearing a blue dress with white polka dots, a light blue apron with flour marks in the shape of hands, black slippers, and thick, curly black hair pulled back into a puffy ponytail. Her skin had a mild glow from sweat, and her eyes showed a radiant kindness that someone would feel from their grandparents during the holidays.

BG called out to the woman. "Can I buy this bear claw?"

The woman looked over from the middle of the store. Her radiance faded once she looked at him. "How did you get in here?"

The kids in the store looked confused, BG most of all. "I'm sorry?"

The woman became indignant. "I said… how did you get in here?"

"Um… I walked through the door with my friends."

"Who are your friends?

BG pointed to Aida and Marcus, who were standing closest to BG in the office. The woman looked over to Aida and Marcus, still indignant. "Is this true?"

Aida and Marcus shrugged at each other, unaware that there would be any problems once they came into the inn. "Yeah, sure, he's cool with us." Marcus replied cheekily as he flicked a smile toward the lady.

"Cool? As in cold?"

"No, cool. Like, he's alright with us. He's our friend."

The lady was not fully convinced but accepted the explanation reluctantly. "Okay." She pointed dismissively towards Luke, who had been looking through the newspapers on the shelf. "Is *he* with you too?"

Unsure as to why she was so mad, Marcus was hesitant. "Uh… yeah, he's with us too."

The lady then marched over to Aida and Marcus. She

ignored Marcus and stared directly at Aida. The shopkeeper stood four inches away with a deathly stare. This made Aida extremely uncomfortable. Aida rolled her eyes toward Marcus with terror and uncertainty.

"Look at me," the lady commanded Aida. "Let me look at you." Aida complied, allowing herself to be probed by the cutting gaze of this woman. The woman looked into Aida's eyes in the same way that the child did, looking for something but unable to understand what she was looking for. After several seconds, the lady's expression softened from skepticism to curiosity, to acceptance and almost loving.

"I'm so sorry for that. You're more than welcome to be here as well." She spoke kindly to Aida.

Slightly annoyed, she gave a resigned "thanks" while looking back at the woman to understand what just happened.

Marcus looked back at the lady. "So, is everyone okay to stay?"

The lady turned and looked up at Marcus. "Hmm? Oh yes, everyone else seems like they'll be okay. So long as you and your lady friend can vouch for everyone here." She pointed toward Luke and BG. "Especially those two."

Without missing a beat, Marcus flashed a smile. "You've got it." She started walking away until he called her back with another question. "By the way, ma'am, what's your name?"

The lady turned and responded. "Oh, how silly of me. My name is Esther."

"Nice to meet you Esther. I think we saw your daughter outside. Dottie, I think?"

"Ah yes, my sweet Dorothy. I'm glad you two are getting along." She walked away with a polite smile as she tended to the various items on the shelves. BG interjected, "So, can I buy this bear claw?"

Esther looked over to BG. "Bear claw?"

"Yes, this pastry. This is a bear claw, right?"

"Bear claw? Hmm... that *is* a good name for that. Yes, that's a bear claw."

"Um, okay. So, can I buy this?"

"As long as..." She stopped herself mid-sentence. Esther looked back at Marcus and Aida. "I'm sorry, I didn't catch your names."

"Oh, I'm sorry. My name is Aida, and this is Marcus."

"Nice to meet you." Esther looked back to BG. "As long as Aida and Marcus will vouch for you, you are alright to buy this. But don't get pushy."

"Thank you. My name is Brandon, but my friends call me..."

Esther cut him off short. "Oh, I don't need to know that." BG was surprised at the disrespect that he received from this lady. She was capable of polite behavior, but he could not understand why he was unwelcome. He looked over to Aida, who cleared her throat and looked away, and Marcus, who gave BG a smirk and shrugged his shoulder for not being able to charm this shopkeeper.

After the exchange, BG was not eager to buy any more supplies from this woman, but he knew that without a decent amount of food to support his large frame, he would not be very pleasant to be around. He was also dating Lisa, who was athletic and had a high metabolism. She was known around school to clean a plate with her tongue if she got hungry enough. There were even silly rumors of her being so hungry and careless that she would be eating plates and lunch trays by mistake, but the rumors were never proven.

BG grabbed different pastries in his hands - bear claws, biscuits, cakes, and macaroons. He also found a jar of peaches, some dried bananas, and a jar of honey for sweetening coffee and cakes. Marcus found a bag of dried oats, fresh vegetables including carrots and a small head of lettuce, and a single, fresh loaf of bread wrapped in paper on the shelves. He intended to make sandwiches at the lake over the weekend. Aida did not find anything that she was interested in eating from the inn, and her uneasiness in the shop made her lose her appetite. Edmond found a bunch of bananas but nothing else that looked interesting.

Luke was spending his time reading the Papers and Announcements section. In the Papers section, he found old newspaper clippings from a publication called the Valley Chronicle, which detailed the information for a small community called Poplar Valley. There were marriage announcements and wedding ceremonies, funeral announcements, and articles on significant and important people in the area.

Every few issues in the Valley Chronicle would also include a crime report, usually crimes expected in small, rural communities - stealing a pig, petty vandalism, things that would be considered a lower-level misdemeanor.

However, there were several announcements published by the Valley Chronicle that were darker, describing more serious crimes and events that surrounded them. There was one announcement for two young men who stole livestock from a local farmer. Another described "vagrancy and general disturbance of the peace", though there were no specific details on what exactly the person did. Both of those announcements ended in the same way, with the person sentenced to be "hung by the neck until dead" - lynching. A different announcement described another lynching that had already occurred:

> "Thaddeus Wright, guilty of vagrancy and of salacious acts with a white woman of high standing, having been convicted not by a jury of his peers but by the jury of collective reason within our community, was taken from the custody of the sheriff's office to face community justice on June 19, 1899. The fire that has sent this heathen ablaze and onto the next world has sufficiently warmed the hearts and souls of our citizens after our Great Blizzard that left our citizens reeling. The people, in their high wisdom and decency, sought fit to bring retribution to this lowly creature. Our position has always been, and always will be so long as this publication continues to print and so long as our homes stand, that the Negro must remain either in submission of the good God-fearing people of Poplar Valley, of our town held high in Providence, or must be dealt with for the safety of the public and future generations to come."

Luke felt disturbed by what he was reading. He turned to the shopkeeper to understand why something like this was in her store.

"Excuse me, miss?" asked Luke to Esther. "Why do you have these papers here?"

Esther said nothing to him. Luke assumed it was because she did not hear him, so he walked closer to her while holding the disturbing paper.

"Ma'am? Why is this paper in the store?"

Again, Esther said nothing, only glaring at Luke and wondering why he had the nerve to talk to her. She continued arranging canned apples on a shelf.

"Okay…" Luke had a glance of contempt. He walked over to Aida for support. "Hey Aida, she isn't talking to me."

"Smart woman," Aida quipped with a smile.

"I'm serious, it's weird. She doesn't have to be rude."

"Welcome to my world when I go shopping." Marcus was all too aware of being treated rudely wherever he shopped.

"Oh, come on." Luke was getting annoyed with being the butt of each joke. Turning back to Aida, he pleaded, "Take a look at this announcement from something called the Valley Chronicle. Have you heard of it?" Aida shook her head no. "It's talking about a lynching in some place called Poplar Valley. I've never heard of it."

"Poplar Valley? Me neither."

"Well, Miss Esther," Luke sneered with an attitude while pointing his head in Esther's direction, "won't help me. Can you ask her about it?"

"Sure, I can give it a try." Aida looked at the announcements more closely as she walked over to Esther.

"Excuse me, Miss Esther?"

"Why, yes, sweetie?" asked Esther brightly.

"Can you tell me about this?" She lifted the announcement

for Esther to see. Esther adjusted her large, round glasses to look.

"Oh, yes. That was from a few years back. Quite a shame. I remember the boy. He wasn't in town for very long, and he was looking for work between the Valley and Lincoln. That was a tough year, with the blizzard and all. The folks around the town were looking for something to celebrate, some event to be a part of. The folks across the way in Lincoln, they were having parties and carrying on. But in the Valley? They decided that they were going to celebrate by grabbing someone from out of town and turning them into one of their own fireworks."

Aida's was looking increasingly distressed about the stories. Aida thought, *Is this woman crazy or senile? A few years back? The Valley and Lincoln? Where did she think this was? When did she think this was?*

Esther continued her story. "When they found that boy, he was tied up with the rope hanging really high on one of the branches. He looked like he had burned all the way through, and the smell was unbearable. Took forever to get him untied. The body was unclean, and there was too much concern about where the body would have to go next.

Most folks around the Valley wanted to just dump it in a hole around here, but a few boys from Lincoln got word of it and decided to give a proper burial."

Aida was stunned and visibly distraught. "My God, that is awful. How did you know about all this?" Esther's next words sent shivers across Aida's skin.

"Because I saw the whole thing happen on that big cottonwood tree outside."

Chapter 4

May 15, 5:39 PM

While Aida spoke to Esther, Marcus sat with Dorothy. "Hey Dottie, how are you?"

"I'm doing quite well, thank you," Dottie replied precociously.

"What are doing?"

"I'm drawing."

"Oh, I really like drawing. Can I see what you're doing?"

"Well, I'm not sure… *can* you?" Dorothy insisted on precision and decorum.

"Ah, I see. *May* I see your fine drawings, my lady?" He bowed with one hand to his chest and his other arm pulled out to his side, and he exaggerated this statement to the point of mockery. Dorothy continued drawing, but she was tickled by the formality.

"Why yes, you may see."

She handed Marcus a stack of paper. On the top of that stack was a pencil sketch of several animals in a row, all in various poses. The drawing was crude but could be considered remarkable for someone of her age.

"Hey Dottie, this looks really nice. I see you made a lot of great animals."

"Thank you very much!" Dorothy was proud of her work.

"Can you tell me what the animals are doing?"

"Of course!" Dorothy pulled Marcus over to a set of three child-sized chairs against a wall near the cash register. She sat on one of the end seats, while Marcus, being a broad and tall individual, had to sit across the two remaining rickety wooden chairs to balance himself. He bent forward to make sure that he could see everything she wanted to show him, and so that he would not fall over.

"So here's an owl. She's really smart and flies really fast." The owl was standing next to a tree. "She's going to be lonely, though."

"Why is she going to be lonely?"

"Because her friends are going to leave."

"Why would they leave?"

Dorothy ignored the question. "And do you see the next one? That's a snake that's hanging upside down from the tree." The snake had a triangular smile on his face.

"What is that in the snake's mouth?"

"He's got some money in his mouth. He was not a very nice snake."

"Why does he have money?"

Dorothy sighed and became a little annoyed with all the questions. She answered in an adorable and exasperated way. "Do you want me to tell you about the rest of the animals or not?"

Marcus chuckled slightly, putting his hand on his chest and feigning as if taken aback by her boldness. "Oh, I'm sorry, my lady. Please continue."

"Thank you." She turned back to the other animal drawings. "This one is a bird. She's really fast and is flying away, but she's going to come back home soon. And this one is a brown bear. He's really nice, and the other animals like him. He's really hot because of all that fire." The bear was in the middle of a blazing fire, with curly pencil marks around him.

"Ah, I can see that. Why is the bear inside the fire?" Dorothy ignored the question.

"This one is a crocodile. He's big and strong, but he has a really big scar in his body because someone got him."

"Wow, that's unfortunate. I like crocodiles."

Dorothy looked up at him with her large, innocent eyes. "I

know, he's my favorite."

"Well, if he's your favorite, then why does he have to have a scar in his body?"

"The monkey did it." And next to the crocodile, was a monkey, trapped in a large circular object. Marcus felt a bit of a chill when Dorothy mentioned the monkey attacking the crocodile, but he was not sure why. He asked about the rest of the picture.

"Why does the monkey's body look like that?" The monkey was stuck inside the barrel, and there were small circles drawn on his body, like he had holes pierced in him.

"He's trying to get out, but he's trapped inside a barrel. He's going crazy in there, but his head and feet are still sticking out. There's his tail too."

"Oh wow, I see it. It's a barrel of monkeys!"

Dottie looked up at Marcus. "What do you mean?"

"You know? It's a barrel of monkeys?"

Dottie stared at him with her head cocked to the side with a blank stare. "I've never heard of that."

"Really? It's like a little game where you have to connect a bunch of little plastic monkeys together. The game is really fun, so when something is fun, they say it's like a barrel of monkeys."

"Plastic… monkeys? Well, there's only one monkey. And I've never seen that before. Is that something from where you come from?"

"Well, I don't live very far from here. Around twenty or thirty minutes down the road in Lorro."

"What's… Lorro? Where is that?"

"That's the city I live in. It's not that far from here. You don't know about Lorro?"

"I don't know. I guess I don't leave very much. I usually just stay around the Cottonwood. Never really had any desire to go too far from here. Plus, I hear it's dangerous."

"Well, every place can be a little dangerous, but Lorro is really nice. You and your mom should visit sometime."

Dorothy sat still and stared blankly at Marcus. "I'm sorry, but I don't think my mom and I will be able to come visit. We have too much keeping us here, and we can't get away from it anytime soon. At least not until our work is done."

"Well, I don't know when you can get everything done around here," he mocked as he looked around the small, dirty inn, "but, if you ever make it, you and your mom should call me and hang out." Marcus took the paper and wrote down his telephone number.

"Wow, you have a telephone? That's amazing! You must be very important. We have to use the town phone about a mile away. I'll be sure to get over there and call if we ever finish up."

Marcus could not understand why she was so excited about his family having a telephone. Looking at the inn and hearing how she was reacting, he concluded that she was poor, the type of poor that he was not accustomed to being around. He thought of the type of poverty that his parents had always feared and warned him about. Marcus's parents always instilled a sense of pride in their position in life, that they worked hard for their privileges, and they were always worried that one mistake could bring everything crashing down. He did not want this for anyone, and he certainly did not want it for this little girl in front of him. He looked at her empathetically, with a softer voice. "I hope you do."

The group continued to shop for a few more minutes to gather goods for their trip. In addition to BG's pastries and jars of juice, they bought extra paper tissues to be used as both napkins and emergency toilet paper before they got back on the road. Their experience in the inn was a little unnerving, and they wanted to get out as soon as possible to hit the road and enjoy their weekend.

"Before you go, I've got something for you all." Esther, who had been putting their items into two discolored paper bags. She pulled a jar filled with a creamy white substance from underneath the table that held her cash box.

Edmond was interested. "What is this? It looks like mayonnaise." He had been trying to keep a low profile during the stop.

Esther was weirdly excited to give them the jar. "It's delicious. In addition to all the different things he does, our friend out back makes it special for us."

Aida looked around. "Which friend? We didn't see anyone other than your daughter around here."

"Oh, he comes in and out from time to time. He usually keeps to himself and takes care of things around the grounds. Tends to the tree outside, makes barrels and jars, sometimes a bit of light carpentry to fix our tables and shelves. And when he has some time, he makes us some delicious treats - mayonnaise, mustard, several types of preserves, lots of things. Whatever I tell him to make. For you, I offer this as a gift. Make sure that everyone who deserves it can get a taste for whatever food you plan to eat."

"Thanks so much" Marcus flashed his signature smile. "I don't know why anyone deserves mayonnaise or mustard, but we'll be sure to use this."

"Well, our particular blend is unique. An acquired taste. I figure at least a couple of you will be able to enjoy it."

"I'm sure we will, ma'am," assured Aida.

Esther turned back to the kids to collect her payment. After a quick glance at the items, she tallied the total in her head. "Okay, that will be four dollars and fifty cents."

Marcus walked over to Luke, then put his arm around him.

"Listen, buddy. I forgot to bring my wallet in from the van. Can you cover this for now and I can pick up stuff on the way back?" Luke turned to Edmond to see if he could foot the bill.

"Uh, yeah, I left mine too."

"I'm just broke right now," BG uttered as he was ferociously eating one of the bear claws.

Luke gave a disgusted glance at his friends as he pulled out his wallet from his pocket, peeled a twenty-dollar bill from a short stack of cash, and handed it to Esther. Esther would not take the bill directly from his hand, giving him an even more disgusted look. Seeing her face, he gingerly placed the bill onto the counter, and Esther quickly snatched it, not breaking her gaze from Luke until he was safely away from her. She looked at the bill and got angry.

"What is this?"

Luke answered, slightly irate. "It's a twenty."

"This is Andrew Jackson's face. This is the devil's bill. I will not accept it. This will NOT be accepted!" She threw it on the floor in front of them. "Why is he on this?"

"Because… that's a twenty." It was strange that he had to defend a money denomination.

Esther pulled the bags away and put them behind the counter. "I won't take it. You can leave without buying anything."

"Oh, come on! It's real money."

"I won't take it!"

Aida, remembering that she keeps extra cash in her sock for emergencies, intervenes in the argument.

"Wait, wait, is your problem just that we're using that bill?"

"Yes, I won't take anything with that man's face on it."

"Okay, I just remembered that I have some extra money. I'll just give you that." Aida goes into her sock and pulls out thirty-five dollars. She peeled away one ten-dollar bill and placed it on the counter.

"There you go, does that work, ma'am?"

Esther took the money that Aida left, staring at the pictures on both notes. "Ma'am, I apologize. This is all the money that we have for this trip." Aida did not want to tell a lie, but she also did not want to spend all day arguing over how the woman would get paid.

"Well, I've never really seen this before, but if you don't have any other notes, I guess this looks alright to me. Okay, I'll accept these." She put the money in her cash box and started counting out the change.

"Oh, and you can keep the change." Aida waved her hand.

"Why, thank you dear. I figured you wouldn't be like some of these others that come around here." Whether inadvertent or not, she leaned her gaze toward Luke and partially toward BG, who was just finishing his bear claw and only slightly aware of everything going on around him.

"Um… thank you, ma'am, I guess," whispered Aida.

"Yes, thanks so much." Marcus was enthusiastic. The kids collected their items and walked out of the store, with Esther and Dorothy walking next to each other and following behind the group to see them out the door.

Chapter 5

May 15, 5:53 PM

As the group left the store, BG glanced to the right and saw a man in the distance, not too far from the large cottonwood tree. The man wore a white shirt, which was torn and discolored from years of use, a pair of muddy denim jeans, black boots, and a large, black, wide-brimmed hat that covered the top of his face. He sported a long, gray beard, which covered the bottom half of his face and hung low enough to cover his chest region. Between his hat and his beard, there was only the thinnest area to see his sunken, shadowed eyes. His arms were long and thin, with wiry fingers, and his skin was pale, almost transparent. Although he was extremely slender, the muscles of his arms stretched out and bulged strong, the muscles of a man that had labored for many years. From a distance, his physical presence was a striking contrast to the vibrant colors of the tree and the red clay-like ground beneath his feet.

The man was sitting on a wooden stool, among a variety of carpentry and building items – long pieces of water-soaked wood in buckets, curved blades with wooden handles, iron hoops lying near his feet, and other smaller tools of assorted sizes and shapes. He was scraping one of the curved blades against the edges of a two-by-four block of wood, measuring it against one of the iron hoops.

Edmond asked, "Hey, who's that guy?"

Esther answered as she followed the group outside. "Him over there? Oh, he's the man that I was telling you about. Looks like he's making a new barrel today."

"Do you all have things to put away?"

Aida, Marcus, and Luke looked at Edmond, trying to understand why he would ask something so silly, as if a barrel would be made to do anything but store something. Even BG looked up from his food to shake his head at Edmond in disdain.

"Why, yes. He usually makes barrels when we need to hold something. He seems to be a in a bit of a hurry though. Usually takes him a bit longer to make sure the wood is seasoned properly. He must need it for something soon."

Edmond felt uneasy. "That feels… weird, for some reason."

Esther reassured Edmond. "Oh, I'm sure everything is fine. I'll be looking forward to seeing what he comes up with."

Just then, the man abruptly stopped. He lifted his head

above his work and stood up, over the pile of tools and equipment. With a loud and booming voice, he called out: "Esther, about how many jobs you think I'll have to do this weekend?" His slow, vaguely Irish accent carried through the air.

Esther called back: "Oh, I'd say definitely two."

The man lifted his head and stared back at the group, scanning across their faces. Even from such a long distance, the kids could feel his cold gaze on each of them slowly. After a brief glance, he bellowed back: "Are you sure ma'am? Looks like I'd have to do three jobs today."

"Well, it could be three. Depends on how things go. I'm certain that we've got two jobs to get done, but you should be ready to finish a third job, just in case." She turned to Dorothy. "Dottie, what do you think? How many need to get done today?"

She walked to Esther, holding her piece of paper with the drawing in hand. She held it between two fingers on each hand, as if holding a tiny tray of food. She did not want to wrinkle her hard work. Aida peeked at the drawing as Dottie walked past her to deliver the paper to Esther. Most of the picture was obscured by Dorothy's hand, but she saw the outline of a sad owl as she passed it to her mother.

"Mama, I think it has to be three jobs today." She handed the drawing to Esther. Esther held the drawing close to her face as she slowly examined every line that Dorothy drew on the page. After about fifteen seconds, she handed the picture back to her daughter.

"Thanks baby." She turned back to the man. "She's right, we're probably looking at three."

"Yes, ma'am. I'll be sure to finish my preparations. And once I'm done with those jobs?"

"Well, then, I think you'll be ready to go home."

Aida leaned toward Esther. "What sort of work is he doing this weekend?"

Esther replied, "Oh, he takes care of some odds and ends around the inn. Usually deals with some things that may come up in the surrounding forest." The forested area around the inn was so dense that there was only a sliver of light coming from the trees.

"Looks like he's got some big jobs to take care of, based on all of those tools he has," Marcus observed.

"Oh, nothing he hasn't handled before. He's almost paid off the debts that he owes, and if things go well, these last jobs might wrap things up for him."

Aida was curious. "So, what are you going to do if he's done with all of his work?"

"I'll be relieved once he's done. The sooner he's done with

his business, the sooner we can both just move on, and I can pass everything down to my sweet little Dottie."

"You're going to retire?"

Esther laughed lightly. "Yup, I think that's a good word for it… retirement. But as we all know, we never retire. The struggle continues."

Marcus gave a slight chuckle. "Well, ma'am, we wish you good luck. Hopefully, everything goes well with the projects."

Edmond reiterated, "Yeah, I hope everything will be alright."

"Of course, children, things are going to go exactly as they should." Esther then turned to Aida. "And young lady, it was genuinely nice to meet you. You seem like an intelligent and gifted young lady. I hope you find everything that you've ever wanted."

Aida smiled. "Well, that was extremely sweet. Thank you so much, and all the best to you, ma'am."

"And all the best to you."

Dorothy chimed in. "Hope to see you again, Ms. Aida!"

"Same here!"

The friends took their items into the van. BG sat in the

passenger seat and offered pastries to Lisa, who had been reading comic books in the driver's seat as she waited. Edmond entered the back seat of the van first, followed by Marcus, Luke, and finally Aida. As they entered, Edmond remarked, "Hey, where'd they go?"

The kids looked back to the Cottonwood Inn, realizing that Esther, Dorothy, and the man had all disappeared behind the dust clouds, leaving only the carpentry tools, the large tree, and a dusty facade across red-clayed floor visible from the van.

Chapter 6

May 15, 5:58 PM

"That was weird."

Luke was still weary over the encounter at the Cottonwood Inn. "I have no idea why that woman acted like that. She was so rude, and so creepy."

Marcus was dismissive. "You're being ridiculous. She was a nice lady, and we got what we needed. And at a really good price, too."

"That place was dirty, and that woman was rude. And her daughter was just as weird, too."

BG was eating a croissant with poppy seeds. "I agree, she wasn't very warm to either me or Luke. It was strange. But Marcus is right, the prices were really good."

"Maybe you guys don't have a trusting face," mocked Marcus. "Maybe if you were better looking or more charming, you'd be able to inspire such kindness and affection."

"Whatever. I just don't think she liked white people."

Now Edmond was dismissive. "Are you serious?" He looked to the others for validation, then back to Luke.

"You can't be serious."

"What else explains it?" asked Luke. "I mean, come on, she didn't want us there. Even her daughter didn't want to be near us."

"You're being stupid again," Aida had been trying, and failing, to enjoy the beautiful landscape over Route 87 during the rest of their trip to the lake. "I'm white, and she was really nice to me."

"Maybe it's because you're a girl."

"Maybe it's because I'm not an asshole."

"Excuse your language, *Miss* Aida. I'm telling you, she didn't want us there."

Lisa interjected. "Guys? I have a question. Does anyone have anything sweet?" BG went into a bag, took out a small chocolate pastry, and handed it to her.

"Thanks, babe." She popped the pastry in her mouth and talked through her chewing. "Now, no more arguing, people. We should be there in about thirty minutes. Next stop, Minstrel Lake."

Minstrel Lake was a forty-seven square mile lake, located about eighty-six miles west of Lorro. The lake was a favorite spot for young, high-school-aged kids from the local surrounding areas. They would congregate and enjoy time away from their studies and families, as well as engage in young romance - innocent walks around the lake's sizeable walking trail, snuggling near one of three fire pits, random trysts among strangers or students from rival schools, sharing their first "special time" on prom night. Intertwined with the walking path that surrounds the lake was an expanse of trees, along with a few empty cabins, each with standard plumbing built for public use and special lockers for protecting gear from both strangers and local wildlife.

The cabins served on a first come-first serve basis, and without any formal monitoring by staff or police, overnight visitors took it upon themselves to ensure cleanliness and orderly use of the space. The cabins themselves were modest, with only four beds set up as a pair of bunk beds and basic plumbing, including indoor bathrooms and a single sink. The local municipality left large plastic trash bags for people to collectively clean the area, and groundskeepers came periodically, though they were not always available.

Marcus shook his head. "You know I've never been comfortable with the name of this place."

"Here we go again." Luke rolled his eyes.

"I'm serious, man. I just picture a bunch of random people in blackface dancing around with pennies being thrown at them."

"Or even WORSE, Black people in blackface." Luke had a small chuckle from this idea.

"That's not funny." Marcus was agitated and ready for another round of arguing.

"Don't worry," Aida interjected. "I read all about it a while back. This place was named for the Italian minstrels that performed shows as they passed through. The name is just a coincidence." The lake had indeed been named for the travelling musicians that came from southern Italy in the late 1800s and early 1900s. They were noticeable, because there were not many Italian immigrants that travelled around the American South during that era, let alone those that were avid musicians.

"Really?" asked Marcus, surprised. He thought he had known most things about most things.

"Yeah, and I should know. I keep up with my ancestors too." Aida gave a smug smile to Marcus. He smiled back, knowing that he had been bested.

The kids pulled into the large driveway of the lake grounds. The driveway encircled one of the cabins at the lake, which also boasted a very sizeable lawn. There were wildflowers and daffodils filled along the grass, with intermittent dusty patches from the tents of previous campers. The remaining two cabins were located between the driveway and the lake, with different types of trees and the main running path set up in the buffer between the two.

Although they arrived at the lake with plenty of daylight to spare, there were already several cars parked around the campgrounds.

Edmond scoffed. "Dammit, we didn't make it early enough. I told you we should have left sooner."

Luke chastised him, "So what? You still would have forgotten to pack our food."

BG turned his head. "Guys… please stop. Just be quiet for a few minutes and enjoy what you get to see. We may not get another chance to take this all in again."

It was true, the view around Minstrel Lake was stunning. The lake had been known historically as a place of great inspiration for weary travelers and a sanctuary of comfort for those that felt unsafe. Black people of the American South and indigenous Americans that lived in the area were always treated with hostility.

Depending on how recently you immigrated from Europe, you could be a target for a variety of abuses by those who came just a generation or two before. With some shared stories among them, many of these same groups used Minstrel Lake as a place of refuge and peace - exchanging goods, assisting each other in finding the next safe place along the road, or helping transport individuals to safety.

The lake was a common passageway for the Underground Railroad, those avoiding the forced relocation and starvation during the Trail of Tears, and recent immigrants travelling along the Gulf Coast from Florida to Texas. Much like the students, the previous travelers also used the lake as a place for evening rendezvous. Some even used the lake and surrounding forest for secret weddings or giving birth away from dangerous places. Many of these stories were engraved in plaques around the running trail and on the cabins.

Lisa stopped the car along the circular driveway, near the center of all of the cabins, and everyone exited the car and unloaded their bags for the weekend.

Marcus retrieved his duffel bag from the car. "Aida, I know that this place isn't supposed to be offensive, but it's still a bit weird."

Aida shot him a smirk. "Relax. Don't worry. if you feel unsafe, I'll be sure to protect you." Marcus smiled back.

Meanwhile, BG was planning accommodations with Lisa. "Where do you want to set up, babe?" The two of them brought their own sleeping bags and equipment, including secret candy bars that they kept hidden from the group.

"I don't know. We can set up on the front lawn." Lisa started cleaning the floor of the van, checking for any loose items.

"Wait, you guys don't want to stay in one of the cabins?" asked Edmond, who was taking his bag out of the trunk. "I thought we were all staying together." Edmond felt his anxiety rising when he realized that he did not bring all of the necessary equipment for this trip.

"Nah, we wanted to get some quality time together in the evening. We can still hang out during the day, but we'd still like to take some time with each other." Lisa tried to remain firm yet diplomatic with Edmond. He did not seem to understand the direction of the conversation.

"But why? What are you planning to do?"

"We have sex," BG said flatly from beyond the other side of the van. He slowly walked around to meet Lisa and Edmond. BG spoke to them in a matter-of-fact tone. "We are planning to spend our time hanging out with you, talking with you, reminiscing over our time together these last four years, for every moment that this warm sun is bathing over this beautiful landscape and across this glistening lake. And then, in the evening," he continued as he put his arm around Lisa and pulled her close, "I plan to snuggle up to my beautiful lady and enjoy some private time before I go to bed. Will that be all right with you?"

Edmond shivered with discomfort. He picked up his bag of clothes and food and quietly walked away toward one of the cabins.

Lisa and BG looked at each other with a small giggle. Lisa called back to the others in the group. "What is everyone else planning to do?"

Marcus shrugged. "I don't know, probably try to get into one of these cabins. I brought my sleeping bag, just in case." He lifted his bag to show the group.

Meanwhile, Aida's eyes were darting around the floor of the van. "Oh, I think I forgot mine." She started looking around the van to see if she was mistaken.

"Don't worry about it, you can use mine if you need to."

"Thanks so much, Marcus. That's very sweet, but I think I'll be okay."

"Alright, just let me know if you need any help."

Luke, not wanting to be shunned, and trying a way to find comfort with Aida for the weekend, interjected in the conversation. "Hey Aida, you can use my sleeping bag too."

"Uh, thanks Luke. I appreciate it." Aida rolled her eyes. She was not excited for this idea.

"Yeah, and if it's not warm enough, I can try and help you with maximizing the efficiency of the sleeping bag."

Aida tried to hide her wincing. "Oh, that's okay. I think I'll be fine with my own arrangement if it's all the same to you." Now she was visibly uninterested.

"Alright, just let me know." Luke flashed a large but unsure smile on his face. Aida responded with one eyebrow lifted with her face contorted, a confused look. Luke's smile slowly faded away, and soon the rest of him faded into the background.

Edmond went to one of the interior cabins away from the lakeside to see if there was any space for anyone. He went to knock on the door, only to see that it was open and there were sounds coming from inside. He recognized the voices coming from the cabin - members of the audio-visual club at Lorro High School.

He walked in with a loud "Hey!" against the sounds of cheering, laughing, and carrying on. Edmond was a member of the audiovisual club from the beginning of his sophomore year until the middle of his senior year, when his anxiety started to become more serious and he had to quit the club. Since he had an alternate class schedule, he had not seen them for a few months. Seeing his comrades filled him with joy, a happiness that he did not always feel with his current friends. He finally found where he was going to stay for the weekend.

Meanwhile, Luke, Marcus, and Aida were trying to secure their accommodations. After collecting their clothes and food, the trio went into the cabin closest to the van. Marcus and Aida walked into the cabin, which looked like a complete disaster. The stench of stale beer and adolescent sweat hit their noses swiftly, making them wince in disgust. The cabin had four beds, all of which had mattresses overturned and liquid stains of various colors spread across them. Old shaving cream was smeared into the walls. A desk lamp had been knocked over with a broken bulb still in the lamp's socket. The cabin floor was littered with plastic cups and paper towels, and rolls of toilet paper were thrown on every piece of furniture.

"Ugh, what is this?" Aida felt a sinking feeling in her stomach as she took a few steps in.

"Looks like someone had a good time," Marcus quipped sarcastically. "Hopefully, they saved some fun for us." He stepped into the cabin, gingerly avoiding the mess.

Luke remained outside the door. "This type of fun? No thanks. I think I'm going to check out the other cabin."

Marcus was staring hesitantly over the multi-colored stained beds. "Yeah, I think this place isn't happening."

"Maybe, we can try and clean the place up?" Aida was hopeful.

Marcus looked to see what Aida's crooked face was looking at. She was looking down at a pile of condoms laying on the ground. Some were still in their original packaging. Others were not.

"Never mind. Absolutely not."

Aida and Marcus walked out of the cabin, avoiding any of the sloppy mess strewn about. They walked over to the third cabin which was a bit further down the lakeside. Luke ahead of them.

"So, what are you planning to do while we're up here?" asked Marcus.

"Just take in all that nature. Get a bit of quiet time, do some reading. Probably do a little running with Lisa. I've got to stay in shape for college tryouts. What are you trying to get into?"

"Nothing."

"Nothing?"

"Absolutely nothing. I have been doing too much this year. School work, student council, continuing to stay this cool." As usual, Marcus was impressed with himself. As usual, Aida was less impressed. "For once, I'd like to enjoy the last few days of senior year leaving everything alone and doing absolutely nothing." He held very hard emphasis on *absolutely*.

"Yeah, that's a good point. I can respect that. I wish I could do the same. I know that if I stop running, even for a little bit, I might not get that scholarship. I might literally fall behind." Aida had been competing for a track and field scholarship to college, and she needed to stay in shape to compete. She was confident in her ability, but not always confident in her focus. "Especially if I'm competing against Lisa for scholarship money. She's amazing."

"She's fairly good, I guess, but you're good too. I've seen you run. You're fast."

"Don't get me wrong, I'm *really* fast, but there's always something that keeps me from getting ahead. Last year, Lisa and I were right next to each other in a two-hundred-meter dash, and my brain went somewhere else in the last second. She got the gold, and I took home silver. We still beat everyone else by a mile, but I wish I could just stay focused long enough to win."

"Well, I wouldn't worry too much about that. You'll figure it all out. You're going to make it in whatever you're trying to accomplish. I believe in you."

"Thanks, Marcus. But I think we'll all make it, one way or another."

"Eh, I'm not so sure sometimes."

Aida was surprised at his lack of smug confidence. "What do you mean? You've got everything going for you."

"Yeah, that's true," he said with a faint smile. "I'm pretty great. But in all seriousness, I worry every day."

"How come?"

"There aren't a lot of opportunities around here for me to really succeed. Georgia is nice, but I'd like to travel around the world and see the sights. Speak to people in different languages, climb mountains, feel sand from the beaches in Europe. And I know that there could be that one person that doesn't want me to make it, or even someone that might be having a hard day and just decide that they need to take it out on me, and that's it for me. Even now, I'm not sure if I'm going to see anything exotic or visit any new places that far from Lorro."

"Don't say that. We're all going to get out of here. You, Edmond, BG, even someone as irritating as Luke will figure it out."

"Yeah, but I know they'll be okay. Edmond's family can hook him up with a job at the store if they need to. BG is a nice enough guy, so he can get by anywhere. Luke, he's rich and white, so he can be as annoying and mediocre as he wants to be, and someone will look out for him."

"Well, I'm white and nothing is guaranteed for me."

"Yeah, but you're different."

"And how am I different?"

"I've seen you put in the work. You and your sisters are always keeping it together. Your family is so warm and welcoming. You've got something special."

Aida was touched and started blushing. "That is really sweet, Marcus. I'm happy you said that."

"And it helps that you're good looking."

Aida stopped blushing. "Marcus… don't do that."

"What? You're objectively pretty. You should use that."

"Marcus, I'm not going to fall for your charms. I'm not interested."

"I'm not interested, either." Aida was slightly taken aback. "Our families are too close at this point. You're more like a sister to me. Besides, you should be fortunate enough to be as pretty as me."

Aida smirked. "You know, you're not as clever as you think you are."

"You're right, I'm way more clever than I think I am."

Marcus and Aida had been close, about as close as any two people could be. As far back as elementary school, Aida and Marcus had played together, worked on school projects together, and supported each other in any way they could. When Aida had to train for competitions or study on math exams, Marcus made sure to help her after school. When Marcus needed help with a school election or a history project, Aida would return the favor. Even their parents knew each other from civic groups, parent-teacher conference days, and other activities around town. Marcus always saw Aida's mother as an auntie, and Aida saw his parents as her second set of parents.

During those times, Aida forged a special bond with Marcus's father, who was always there to share some fatherly advice or a corny joke with them.

Marcus and Aida finally caught up to Luke in front of the third cabin. Luke tried to open the cabin door, only to find the door locked.

Luke was incensed. "Aw, come on! I want to get settled somewhere."

"Maybe you should have remembered your sleeping bag, and then you wouldn't be so worried." Aida had known Luke for many years, and he was known for being unprepared and somehow finding a way out of a bad situation. Typically, one of his friends would show him mercy or find a way to include him into their plans. So when Luke started complaining, Aida was not surprised.

"I have the sleeping bag in the van. I just thought I could toss it on a bed instead of sleeping on the ground. I don't like sleeping on the ground."

Marcus stopped, confused. "Wait, this is a camping trip.

You knew there was a chance that you might sleep on the ground, and you didn't think about sleeping on the ground?"

Luke knocked on the door. "I wasn't worried about that. Besides, I think this will work out."

Just as there was a pause in the conversation, two sixteen-year-old girls opened the cabin door, both dressed in shorts and comfortable, bright-colored tank tops - appropriate clothing for a late spring day in Georgia.

"Yes, can we help you?"

The girls were beautiful, with sunny, smiling faces that could light up a room. Luke tried to find the words, but he was incapable of civil conversation with beautiful girls at a moment's notice, so Aida spoke before he could embarrass himself.

"Hello! We were just looking for a place to stay for the night, but it looks like this cabin is occupied."

One of the girls chimed in. "Well, it's not fully occupied."

"Yeah, it's only the two of us because our friends decided to bail," the other one interjected, "So, we have two extra beds if you all want to join."

Aida, Marcus, and Luke looked at each other. Luke was excited about the possibility of spending the night with the two girls. Marcus was curious but could be convinced either way. He was popular and interesting to be around, so he did not have any problems attracting new friends, let alone pretty girls. He never felt any pressure to impress anyone. Aida was concerned about being in a single cabin with Luke and two other random girls.

Recognizing the whims of teenage boys and choosing not to be a part of it. "It's okay, I'll just stay in the van tonight."

"We couldn't possibly do that, Aida." Marcus feigned concern, though he was hoping that Aida would get the hint.

"Of course, we can!" exclaimed Luke, sounding uncomposed, obvious, and desperate. He turned to see the bent, quizzical expressions on his friends' faces and the young lady that opened the door.

However, the second girl appeared more open to Luke staying with them. He saw her face and relaxed. "I mean, there's no point in wasting the space, especially over such a nice weekend." Marcus and Aida rolled their eyes, but both were also impressed with the way Luke managed to save his ego this time.

"I guess it's okay if it's alright with Erica," said the blonde girl as she looked back at her friend.

"Yeah, that works for me, Stacy." She smiled again at

Luke.

"Well, alright then. We can just get settled and try not to bother you too much." Luke felt more relaxed, but also aware to keep conversation light and easy-going. As he and Marcus started bringing their bags into the cabin, Marcus turned around to Aida.

"Are you sure you're okay with staying in the van tonight?"

"Absolutely. You kids have a fun time." She exaggerated like her dad, in the silly way he liked to speak when he knew he was embarrassing his children.

"Thanks Aida, this means a lot. I'll pay you back one day."

"Just remember when you pay me back, spell my name right on the check." Aida smiled at Marcus, again in the embarrassing way that her father would smile at her. He smiled back. The door closed in front of her, and Aida stood in front of the cabin, briefly taking in all of the beauty and quaintness of the scenery before she picked up her bag and walked it back to the van.

Aida settled into the van, did some light reading from one of her history books, and took a quick nap.

The nap came at an opportune time since a brief but strong storm came through. The rain came down in squalls for a while, and the storm winds knocked over several tree branches. The people in the cabins did not feel it too much, but the storm made the van shake and tremble. Aida did not usually sleep well, but the storm made her feel calm. She spent her time around a lot of people. At home, she was around her parents and three sisters, all of whom had their own activities and lives they led. Being in a modest-sized single-family house did not allow for much privacy. At school, she was always moving from class to class during the day, where she often saw Marcus, BG and Edmond trying to avoid Luke. This was followed by track practice after school, where she and Lisa met and bonded.

She loved her friends and family, but the constant movement of people around her made it difficult for her to have space to think. She had developed an insular personality, which no one realized due to how active she was. If she could have remained on the school's track team without a "team" around, she would have. So she took every chance she could get to sit with her thoughts and clear her mind, enjoying the sounds and the stillness. She was excited to be away from her house for a couple of days. She was even more relieved to have the van all to herself that night, relishing the silence and calm. She reminded herself to thank Stacy and Erica for taking the boys away.

She woke from her nap after twenty-five minutes, feeling refreshed and ready for the rest of the day.

She changed into her track practice clothing - a light, white cotton t-shirt, blue athletic shorts cut just above the knee for freedom of movement, and bright sky blue and white running sneakers that matched her school's official colors. She hopped out of the van and started her stretching routine, admiring the sunset against the backdrop of the trees along the lake. Behind her, Lisa was walking up, also in her running clothes, almost identical except for wearing a pink t-shirt, but still wearing the same shorts and shoes.

"You almost ready?" Lisa called out as she walked up to Aida.

"Yeah, just want to get one last stretch in. Are you all set up?"

"Yup, just got everything put away, including Brandon." Lisa was the only one that called BG "Brandon". Even the teachers did not call him by his real name. Everyone felt comfortable with BG. 'He's asleep in the tent."

"Why is he asleep so early?"

"He's just tired."

"How'd he get so tired? It's not like we did anything yet. Is he okay?"

"He's fine. He just… had a long week and didn't get a lot of sleep last night." Lisa was trying to avoid any discussion of the sex that she and BG just had.

"Oh." Aida figured it out and smirked. "So, it was good then?" Aida wanted the story.

Lisa had been found out. "Well… let's talk about something else."

"Ha, okay." Aida loved to make Lisa uncomfortable, but she was certainly fine with stopping before any juicy details were released. Despite her silent rivalry with her, Aida really liked and respected Lisa, and she liked to engage in playful ribbing. "Where's everyone else?"

"Edmond ran into some people he knows, so he's hanging out in that other cabin. I don't think I know anyone there. I walked past a cabin and heard Luke and Marcus, but it sounds like they're just arguing about something pointless again."

"I'm sure those girls they're staying with aren't enjoying it."

"Wait, they're staying with some girls? Is that why you're sleeping in the van?"

"No, not really. I like having the space to myself, so it's better for me this way. I'd rather be in the cabin by myself, but this can be just as good."

"If you want to join us in our tent space, you can come hang with us."

"I think I'll be okay. Plus, I don't want to get in the way of your special time." Aida slyly smiled as she put her arm around her friend. Lisa blushed. "We should do this run." Lisa agreed, and off they went.

The girls started with a light jog toward the dusty path that surrounded the lake. They weaved through trees that survived across generations - laurel, oak, sassafras, flowers interspersed in bushes near the trail. Slowly, Aida started increasing her stride, trying to pass ahead of Lisa. Not to be outdone, Lisa began increasing her stride as well, smiling at Aida as she moved past her.

Within moments, the two young ladies were in a full sprint, testing their limits and each other's limits. They ducked under branches, hopped over sticks and rocks, weaved around debris, and strafed around bushes and gnats. They passed the Leyli, named for the old, broken wooden trail marker, showing an arrow marked "Ley" in one direction and "Li" in the opposite direction. They ran for about one thousand meters, running past a group of rowdy peers that included Edmond, and Lisa took a quick slowdown to wave to BG, who had finally walked out to the lake to enjoy some alone time. Near the end of their run, Aida fatigued and began to slow down. Lisa had not noticed the slowdown and continued to run about thirty additional meters before turning around to see her friend sore, panting, and bent over.

"Are you okay?" asked Lisa, who was panting a bit, but

continued to run in place.

"I'm alright, I'm just used to shorter running. Can we just sit for a quick second?"

"Sure, let's do it."

Aida and Lisa walked over to a short bench back toward the Leyli, between several freshly planted trees, each around four feet tall and shaped like bushy green cigars. This area was distinctive, as it was the only place at the lake that had such an intentional setup, while the rest of the lake perimeter was part of the original landscape and had only mild tending. For this reason, this bench area functioned as a common milestone for visitors.

Aida sighed as she sat down on the bench, talking in between breaths. "Whew, you're so good. I don't know how you can run so fast for so long. You can't be stopped. It's like you're gliding through the air."

"Thanks, but you kept right up with me." Lisa was breathing calmly at this point.

"Up until I couldn't. I know I'm okay, but I want to get to where you are. I don't want to keep getting silver medals." Lisa felt awkward hearing about her accomplishment, but there was not much to argue. Aida continued. "And I need to do well for my college tryouts."

"Where are you planning to go anyway?"

"I'm not sure yet, but I think I'll be applying to somewhere in-state. I need to get a job to cover my school fees, so even then I might still try to be a walk-on for the spring semester. What about you? You seem like you didn't want to say earlier."

"I'm going away. To California."

"That's great! But why so far away?"

"I've got family that lives in Los Angeles, so I plan to stay with them for a while. I think I need a break from Georgia"

"Really nice. Sunny weather, beautiful people. It should be a fun time. What does BG think of all this?"

"Brandon is okay with it. He wants to take the year off to make money, and you know that his grandmother isn't doing well, so he plans to visit her down in south Florida. He plans on coming out to L.A. in the second year. And I plan on coming back here to visit a few times a year."

"Cool. I'm glad you don't plan to leave forever." She gave Lisa a hug around the shoulders. "Do you and BG have anything else planned for this vacation?"

"Not really. We just wanted to get peace and quiet and have some fun with our friends… and *Luke*." Lisa sneered his name.

"Oh, Luke isn't that bad."

"I know. He's not evil or anything, he's just really annoying. The problem is that he's not so bad that you can tell anyone why you don't want to be around him. He gets obnoxious, and then just when you're completely sick of him, he pulls back, or he says something nice. It makes you look crazy to explain why you don't like him."

"I can see that. He's not like the other meatheads at school. When you're really awful, people can remember that. For some reason, people keep forgetting how terrible he can be."

"That's because people don't forget about his money."

"That's also true. I mean, Marcus's family has money, and he's really nice. BG's family doesn't have as much money as Marcus or Luke, and he's really great. No offense to him, though."

"I don't take any offense, and I'm sure he wouldn't. He's okay with where his family is. I am too. And he's really sweet." Lisa blushed again.

"Do you think that you love him?"

"I really do. He's the love of my life. I just know that I like being with him, and I'm really excited to see where this goes. The best part is that he's willing to travel with me. I want to see the world, fly all over the country and live in every part of it, and I don't think I'd be able to have the strength to do it without him."

"That *is* really sweet. I hope I can find something like that, but I never find anyone that I'd be interested in being with. Not even a little bit. At least not now."

"Really? I thought you might end up with Marcus or something."

"No, not at all. I mean, he's really nice, and he's good looking, but I never felt anything. I think there may be someone in the future, but I'm not stressing over it."

"Eh, it's fine. Everyone has time, and if you choose not to find anything, that's okay as well."

"Thanks for the support." Aida gave Lisa another hug. "Are you ready to get back to this run?"

"Sure. Let's do it!"

The sun started to set as Aida and Lisa stretched. The bright southern sun that shimmered against the lake was disappearing, and the ladies enjoyed the beautiful reds and oranges of the sunset sky. They made sure to get back to the cabins before the sky changed to blue and black.

The kids met one last time at Lisa and BG's camp before they retired to their beds for the night. Luke opted for a sandwich, made with the meat, cheese, and a heavy dose of the mayonnaise spread that they got from the Cottonwood Inn.

Marcus enjoyed a light salad, with the same cheese and a sliced tomato. Lisa had toast and butter, made over a hot plate. BG was trying to lose weight, so enjoyed the same meal, replacing the butter with a light coating of mayonnaise.

Edmond had come to the dinner late and was not able to get more than a handful of crackers. He had mistaken the mayonnaise for some type of cheese spread, which left a very awkward taste in his mouth from the first cracker. After that, he found fruit and cheese to accompany his crackers. Aida did not understand why she was feeling uneasy, but she decided to refrain from eating.

"You're not going to eat anything?" asked Lisa, who was spreading butter on another piece of toast.

"No, I'm alright. I feel funny."

"Are you sure?" Luke's words stumbled out through a mouth full of meat and cheese.

"Yes, Luke, I'm fine." Aida made it clear that Luke's fake concern was unnecessary and unwanted.

"Well, if you want some," he said as he winked and gyrated, indicating a *double entendre,* "just let me know and I can… make you a sandwich."

Aida quickly rebuffed his advance sarcastically. "Okay, I'll be *sure* to do that."

While Luke was being weird toward Aida, Marcus and Edmond decided to play a game that they sometimes played when they were near each other and bored. Marcus pulled out a deck of cards from his bag and selected two at random, a six of clubs and a three of spades.

"Alright, Ed, pick out the clubs." He held them up to Edmond in one hand, not showing the contents. Edmond selected the three of spades.

"Aw, come on, I never get these."

"It's cool man, try again." Marcus selected two more cards, a king of diamonds and a three of diamonds.

"Okay, this one should be easy. Pick out the king." Edmond selected again, and he chose wrong again.

"Come on, man. You have to be messing with me."

"No man, I'm not. See?" Marcus handed the four cards that he selected to Edmond to show him that he was not cheating. "Want to do one more?

"Okay, fine. I've got the next one."

"Okay, buddy. I believe in you." Marcus pulled two more cards. "Okay, man, I've got a diamond and a heart. I want you to choose the diamond."

Edmond rubbed his hands together in anticipation, as if delicately pulling the card would let him pull the right card magically. He slowly took it from Marcus's hand and turned the face to himself quickly. A three of hearts.

"Ah, it's a heart! I'm so bad at this." Edmond threw his hands up in exaggerated despair.

Marcus chuckled to himself. "Man, you'll never get good at this."

"I know, I'm always choosing the wrong thing."

"It's okay about that last one, though." He tossed Edmond the other card. An ace of hearts.

"You suck!" Edmond playfully pushed Marcus's shoulder. "You tricked me. I was gonna get the heart no matter what."

Marcus laughed. "Don't worry man, you'll get it right the next time."

The group finished dinner and agreed to meet at Marcus and Luke's cabin in the morning to get breakfast. Edmond went back to his cabin to talk and get an early night's rest. Luke and Marcus wanted to get back to Erica and Stacy for love connections. Lisa and BG went back to their tent to enjoy alone time. Aida walked back to the van to settle in, covering one of the seats with clothing as makeshift bed sheets and covering the windows to make sure that the moonlight did not keep her awake. She locked the doors, put away her belonging in a safe place, and went to sleep in her running clothes.

A couple of hours later, she woke to a knock on the van door. Being cautious, she grabbed her keys and interlaced them in between her fingers, making sharp points in her fists that jutted from her hand. She did not think there was any danger in such a safe place, but she knew to stay prepared in case any real danger emerged. She thought that it was one of her friends looking for a book or some condoms. However, when she asked, "Who is it?", the voice responded, "Um, it's Stacy. I think I need your help."

Chapter 7

May 16, 1:09 AM

"He's not doing so well." Stacy's heart was racing, her hands were flailing, and she spoke through panic and adrenaline. "We were sitting around trying to have a good time, things were going good. Then all of a sudden, he just started shaking and breathing really hard." Stacy's voice trembled through her explanation.

Aida quickly put on her shoes to leave the van as Stacy continued telling her the situation. "Go on."

"Then he just started throwing up. It was really gross. At first, it was just a little, but then it wouldn't stop. He ran outside and it just kept coming."

"I need to get him out of here now."

As soon as Aida finished putting her shoes on, the two started running back to the cabin.

"Where is he now?" asked Aida through her running.

"He's outside somewhere."

The two girls ran toward the sound of heaving and shuffling near a bush. Luke was bent over on the ground, panting in between expulsions, and unsuccessfully attempting to drink water in between convulsions. He was wearing yellow shorts, a faded gray t-shirt with the band Whitesnake on the front, and a pair of flip-flop sandals, reminiscent of a child.

The girls also saw Marcus and Erica, standing over him frozen in place with no clue what to do next. Erica was wearing light green shorts and a matching bathrobe with matching fuzzy green slippers. Marcus was wearing khaki shorts and a blue Lacoste branded short-sleeved shirt, complete with white athletic shoes and white socks.

"He's been like this for a while now." Marcus handed Luke a towel.

"Geez, Luke, are you okay?" Aida asked.

After letting out a dry heave, Luke screamed out, "Of course I'm not! Why would you ask me that?" He started dry heaving again.

Erica was sweet but oblivious. "He hasn't been doing so well. I think he's really sick." Even in the middle of a crisis, Aida and Marcus rolled their eyes and gave her a dirty look. Even Luke raised his head at Erica to show his disgust at what she just said.

Aida held his head up and looked Luke in the eyes. "Alright, Luke, we're going to take you home."

Marcus agreed. "Yeah, buddy, let's get you back to Lorro."

"Okay, that's fine with me." Luke coughed and let out another heave, which almost forced him to collapse.

Aida and Marcus helped Luke to his feet as Erica and Stacy stood to the side. As they walked Luke back to the van, Marcus called back, "We'll call you sometime, ladies."

Stacy was excited as she lingered on Marcus. "Looking forward to it. We'll be back next weekend."

Marcus nodded at Stacy with a flashy smile then turned to Aida. "Hey, I can take him back to the van. Can you get everyone else so that we can get out of here?"

"Sure thing." Aida removed herself from under Luke's arm and left his safety to Marcus. She ran back to the cabins to get the rest of her friends.

Luke mumbled as he limped under Marcus's support. "No, please don't leave."

Aida reassured him as she ran faster. "Don't worry, I won't be away too long. We're going home."

Luke's voice faded. "Okay, Aida... I'll see you... in a bit..." Marcus continued to drag Luke back to the van.

Aida ran to Edmond's cabin and knocked on the door. An unfamiliar teenaged boy with a Star Wars t-shirt and black shorts answered the door. He spoke very rapidly.

"Hey! How's it going? Oh, you're cute. You want to come in and hang out?" He slurred in between words. He had been drinking before Aida came over.

Aida was agitated and spoke quickly. "No thanks. Is Edmond still around? Can you go get him for me?"

The boy just shrugged his shoulder and called out to Edmond. "Hey Eddie! Some cute girl wants you." Edmond called back from the cabin.

"Really? How cute is she?" The boy turned back to Aida and looked her up and down.

"She's about a seven, maybe an eight. I can't really see as well right now." Aida was not happy at the characterization.

"I'll be right there."

The boy turned back to Aida. "He'll be right there." Aida nodded dismissively. Edmond came to the door, slightly intoxicated, more energetic, and slightly more erratic than usual.

"Oh, it's you. What's going on?"

"Luke's not feeling well, so we need to get back home."

"Whoa, that sucks." Edmond's face exaggerated with fake concern. The two looked at each other briefly.

"So, are we going to go?" asked Aida, tentatively. Edmond was slow to understand what was going on.

"Oh! You want *me* to go, too? Okay, sure, we can go. Just let me do one thing." He grabbed a can of beer, popped the top, and chugged it quickly. Aida waited, tapping her foot in annoyance. "Alright, let me get my stuff. I'll meet you out here."

"Actually, I have to go get Lisa and BG. I'll just meet you at the van."

"Sure, fine." Edmond closed the door and started collecting his things. Aida did not have time to get mad about Edmond's drunkenness and having a door slammed in her face.

Aida ran to the tent where Lisa and BG were staying and called out. "Hey guys, are you awake? You're not… doing stuff, are you?"

BG crawled over to the opening of the tent to see what was going on. "No, we're just reading and cuddling. What's up, Aida?"

"We have to go. Luke is really sick."

BG was disappointed, and it showed on his face. "Do we really have to?"

"BG, he's our friend. We can always come back next

weekend or the weekend after once he gets better. And we used his van, so we should probably go back with him."

"Well, I guess so."

Lisa chimed in. "Do we really, *really* have to?"

"Yeah, I think so, babe. We'll have lots of time this week, so it's no worry." BG had a big heart. As much as Luke irritated him, he was not going to let him stay sick for the trip. However, he also knew that if he fought to keep Luke at the lake, he would complain the whole time and ruin the trip. Coming back the following week would allow him to have time with Lisa without any distractions. "Plus, I just realized that we have the car keys."

"Okay, let me just get some pants on." She reached for a pair of sweatpants.

"I thought you said that you guys weren't doing anything."

"We weren't. I just try not to wear pants if I don't have to. And the sleeping bags we have are really comfy."

Aida was feeling uncomfortable. "Um... okay... well, we're going to be at the van. Just come meet us as fast as you can." Aida turned away and ran back to the van.

Lisa, BG, and Edmond made their way back to the van with their bags and gear. Luke was doubled over and dry heaving while leaning on the back of the van. Marcus was moving back and forth, from slowly rubbing Luke's back and patting it to help him expel whatever was inside.

Aida was going through the van to move her clothes to make space for everyone to get back into the car.

"Geez, man, what's wrong with you?" asked Edmond. Luke slowly lifted his head to give Edmond a dirty look. "Yikes, you look like death."

Aida snapped at Edmond. "What's wrong with you?" She backhanded him harshly on the arm. Edmond pulled back with some mild pain.

"What? I mean, he's looking rough."

Lisa stared at Luke. "He does look pretty bad. I have some water if you need it."

Luke slowly nodded his head and moaned in affirmation. Lisa pulled out a plastic bottle filled with water and handed it to Luke. He started dumping water into his mouth quickly and aggressively, and he managed to mumble a "thank you" in between each gulp. He drank the entire bottle of water and handed the empty bottle back. He then started vomiting again. Marcus started to lift him.

"Alright, buddy, let's get this last one out and get you home. BG, can you help?"

"Sure." BG helped Marcus lift Luke, who continuously groaned and became more lightheaded and delirious. The two lifted his arms over their shoulders and dragged him into the van. Marcus entered first, so that he could secure the middle seat. He and BG then lifted Luke into the van, making sure to secure him near the van's sliding door just in case they needed to pull over.

Next, Edmond got into the seat near the back, trying to avoid the commotion. BG moved into the back seat to help, next to Edmond and behind Luke.

"Hey Lisa, you want me to drive?"

"That's okay, Aida, I can do it." Lisa climbed into the driver's seat. Aida opened the passenger side door and hopped in. Once everyone was inside the van, Lisa turned the key in the ignition, and the van was back on the road back to Lorro.

There were several close calls. Luke almost passed out twice within the first five minutes of the ride, groaning and writhing in pain so unbearable that he began grabbing for the sliding van door, which shifted the weight of the car and caused a panic. He felt like he was going to die. As Marcus and BG tried to wrestle Luke into his seat, BG started complaining about a pain in his stomach as well, which distracted him from keeping an eye on Luke. Moreover, the earlier storm knocked out tree branches all along the highway. The commotion in the van and the road hazards distracted Lisa, and she almost swerved into another oncoming car.

"Lisa, keep it together!" Aida was raising her voice, and she started yelling at the boys in the back to get Luke in line. "What are you guys doing back there?" She turned over her left shoulder to see what the boys were doing.

Marcus was attending to Aida while trying to support and restrain Luke. "We're trying, just relax." Luke continued to flail his arms through Marcus's grip.

BG started to grip his stomach as well. "I don't know man, I don't feel so good, either. I think we may need to pull over."

Edmond started feeling anxious. Dealing with Luke was already too much for him, but he was starting to feel closed in once BG was hurting. "Oh, come on, man. I'm not trying to be a part of this. Move that somewhere else."

"Where else am I supposed to go, you jerk?" asked BG through his mild moans. "This is really happening."

"I don't like this. I really don't like this!"

"Stop screaming!" yelled Aida from the front of the van. "You've got to take it easy."

"I'm trying! But I'm starting to lose it. I'm *really* starting to lose it!"

Lisa interrupted loudly. "Why don't we just stop off at that place we went to earlier? We can get some water, and I think they have some beds in the back."

Aida was skeptical. "I don't think they're going to let us stay for just a few hours."

"Come on, we can probably try. If they don't let us stay, then we can just keep it moving."

Aida quickly conceded. "Fine, let's do it. I don't think it's coming up for a while, but we can try."

No sooner had Aida spoken that the entrance to the Cottonwood Inn emerged through the darkness.

"Hey, that was fast. I thought it was further down." Aida was surprised. Lisa did not normally drive so fast, and even in an emergency, she was surprised that Lisa was able to get back to the Cottonwood Inn so quickly. They would have missed their turn, but for the large tree in front of the building and two lit lanterns at the entrance.

Lisa pulled the van into the driveway, and the kids could see the dusty old building through the faint lantern light. Lisa and Aida jumped out of the car and ran to the front door, surprised to find that the inn is still open.

Aida yelled out to the group still in the van. "Hey! They're still open!" Lisa drove onto the lot and called out for anyone that might still be awake and available.

"Is anyone around? We need some help, please."

Aida called out instructions. "Lisa, go in first. There is a door that leads to a hallway in the back." Lisa stepped out of the car and ran into the Cottonwood, then Aida called back to everyone else. "Guys, let's get Luke out of the van!"

Lisa burst through the front door of the Cottonwood and ran to the back of the store where the doorway to the beds was located. Looking through the doorway, she spotted cracks of moonlight coming through three doors, one to her left near the opening and two to her right a little further away and next to each other. She could barely make out a fourth door on the left, but the door was closed.

"Can we help you?" A small voice echoed from the end of the corridor.

"Who said that?" asked Lisa nervously. The sudden sound of a voice in the darkness struck her with fear. She backed up slowly as she heard footsteps approaching her from the darkness. She did not run away, but she prepared to make a defensive move if she needed. Then, out of the darkness, came an energetic voice and a small face.

"Hi! I haven't met you before. What's your name?"

Lisa eased her shoulders, and her heartbeat began to slow down. She was still confused, but she looked like the little girl that she had seen from the van earlier.

"Oh. Hi, my name is Lisa. What's your name?"

"My name's Dorothy, but my friends call me Dottie. Do you need help with something?"

"Yes, a couple of our friends are extremely sick, and we wanted to know if we could stay here, at least for a little while. Is there an adult around here that can help us?"

A voice called out. "I can help you." Esther emerged from the darkness behind Lisa.

Lisa turned around suddenly. Her heart felt like it jumped into her throat. "Oh! Oh my gosh, I'm so sorry. I didn't see you come up behind me." She grabbed her chest in fear.

"Oh… Lisa, is it? My apologies for frightening you, I was just reviewing our inventory. Had to make sure I had the right count for a special project that I'm working on. I see you've met my daughter Dorothy."

Lisa nodded and smiled but realized that Esther could not possibly have seen her. "Oh, yes, I just spoke with her. She's nice."

"That's because I raised her right. Say, did you come by earlier with those other young people?"

"Yes, the ones in the van. They're outside right now. We stopped off because a couple of our friends got sick and wanted to rest."

Esther turned around to look out the window. In the faint light, she could see the friends climbing out of the van. Aida and Marcus supported Luke's weak body, and Edmond helped a weakened BG walk to the door.

"Ah yes, those are the ones." She turned away from the window and looked at the wall. "Looks like my count was right." She turned back around to Lisa. "I was wondering when you all would return. Of course, you can stay here."

"Thank you so much, Miss Esther. We can stay for a few hours and we'll be out of your way."

"Oh, no worries about that. You all seem like you're in some real trouble." Esther exaggerated her speech. "You can stay here through the night for no charge."

"Really?"

Esther was reassuring. "Yes, no problem. It wouldn't be right to charge you when you're in such a predicament. Now, the rooms don't have any locks on them, but the main doors to the inn will be locked for the rest of the night. Safety first, of course. There is some water near a well in the back, which I can get my assistant to fetch for you. And there should be blankets and pillows for you to use in each room. Maybe a couple of torches too. I assume you'll need all three rooms?"

"Yes, that's perfect, Miss Esther."

"Wonderful." Esther turned to her daughter. "Now Dottie, you know it's late. I think you should attend to something else. The adults will be able to manage it from here."

"Okay, Mama. Nice meeting you, Miss Lisa." Dorothy waved gently and skipped back down the hallway into the darkness.

"Nice meeting you, too."

As Dorothy disappeared into the hallway, the front door of the inn swung open again. The friends stumbled into the inn as they tried to keep their sick friends balanced and attentive. That proved to be harder with each passing moment. "Do you have any available rooms?" asked Marcus while being choked by Luke's arm around the back of his neck.

"Yes, you all can come right this way. The beds are in the back. Be careful not to get caught on anything."

"Thank you, ma'am." They followed Esther's voice to the hallway door and went into the three open rooms. Aida and Marcus pulled Luke into the first room on the left, and Edmond and Lisa brought BG into the first room on the right. Marcus stayed with Luke, and Lisa stayed with BG, leaving Aida and Edmond to take the last available room on the right further down the hallway. Esther called into the hallway, "Say, can you go get some things from outside to take care of these children? A few of them look like they really need it."

"Sure." A grizzled, grumbling voice echoed from behind the closed door. "I'll get right on it." There was the faint sound of shuffling coming from inside the closed room, then the sound of a door opening to the outside.

The healthy friends were reassuring the sick ones that everything was going to be okay.

There were two cots in each room, with older-styled blankets and feather pillows. After several minutes, a bucket of fresh water appeared next to the doorway of each room, from which everyone took a drink. Aida and Edmond went to get food from the main store area, but they found that the food had disappeared. The shelves and tables were all barren. The cash register was not even visible.

"That's strange." Aida did not understand why they would remove everything from the main area, especially when there was a working lock on the front door.

Edmond was not fazed. "Yeah. I wouldn't worry about it though. I think we need to get some food after we sleep for a bit. Besides, I'm still feeling a little anxious and I don't want to fill up before bed."

"It's not for you, Edmond, it's for the others."

"They'll be fine, so long as everyone keeps it together. I'm going to get some sleep." Edmond walked back to their room and collapsed on the cot furthest away from the room entrance. Aida looked behind her while walking back to the room, still confused about why everything was taken away. She set her thoughts aside, checked in with Luke and BG once more to make sure they were drinking plenty of water, and made her way back to her room for a quick nap.

Chapter 8

May 16, 1:32 AM

Luke and BG slept for a couple of hours while Marcus and Lisa took care of them in their respective rooms. They eventually fell asleep themselves, along with Edmond, whose snoring was loud enough to fill the hallway. Aida laid wide awake on her cot, unable to get any sleep due to the snoring. So, she stared at the ceiling, thinking about her plans for her future as a history major and as a track runner. She went through her regiment - read, run at least five miles a day, lift weights, manage a diet plan, develop a strict sleep schedule. Occasionally, she stretched her legs into the air as she stared at the ceiling or twisted her body to stretch her hips and back. Aida was serious about having a career in track and field. Academic and career plans were necessary but secondary - she planned to study history in college, but her true passion was in athletics. She was willing to do anything as long as it gave her time to stay in performance shape and allowed her a flexible schedule.

Aida was restless. She slowly rolled out of her cot, carefully placed her running shoes back on, and sneaked out of the room. She was careful to grab one of the lanterns on a small table near the entrance without anyone waking up. As she walked out of the room, she felt a cold chill run across her back, which she attributed to a drafty hallway. She lifted the lantern to see a closed door in front of her, the room of the mysterious barrel maker that she saw earlier. He was able to retrieve water without coming through the main hallway, so she figured that he had his own exit to the outside. Turning left, she walked to the other rooms to see how her friends were doing. In the room to the left, she saw Lisa asleep in a chair, with her hand draped over the edge of BG's cot. Other than his low, constant groaning, BG was fast asleep, dead to the world. In the room across the hall, she saw Marcus asleep peacefully in his cot with a smile on his face.

Luke was absent from his room.

Aida walked in and shook Marcus's shoulder to wake him. His smile faded as he came back into consciousness.

"Hey, Aida, what's going on? I was dreaming a beautiful dream about the girls."

"Erica or Stacy?"

Marcus smiled. "Yes." Aida sighed and rolled her eyes. "What's going on, Aida?"

"Nothing, I couldn't sleep. Where's Luke?"

"What do you mean?"

"He's not here. Where did he go?"

Marcus was tired and uninterested. "I don't know, maybe he took a walk somewhere."

"Take a walk here? Why would he do that? He's not well."

"I don't know. I'll go check the bathroom." Marcus lifted himself.

"Here, take this. I can wait." Aida handed Marcus the lantern.

Marcus rolled out of his cot and walked toward the bathroom while Aida waited in the darkness of his room. He came back after only a few seconds.

"I didn't see him."

"He's not in the bathroom?"

"I completely forgot, there isn't a bathroom around here."

"That's weird. Maybe he went outside?"

"You can go outside and check for him yourself."

"I'm not going to do that. It's creepy. Can you go outside and check?"

"You want me to risk my life? In the country?"

Aida realized this might not be the safest place for Marcus

to walk around by himself.

"Yeah, I see your point. Take BG and Edmond with you. It's better if you all go." Aida was worried enough, but she was not going to risk going outside herself.

"Yeah, okay, fine." Marcus went into the other rooms to get BG and Edmond. BG was still feeling bad, and the pain was growing worse as he walked outside. Edmond's anxiety had subsided with a little rest, so he would be able to help Marcus carry BG back to his room. They flanked BG as they went outside to find Luke. Aida stayed with Lisa in her room, holding the other lantern.

Not long after the boys went outside, the girls heard a loud collective scream. Aida and Lisa looked at each other to confirm that they heard the same thing, then grabbed the lantern to investigate. The girls stepped out of the inn and saw the boys' lantern floating in the darkness near the large tree, with Marcus's silhouette holding the lantern and the outlines of BG and Edmond next to him. As they moved closer, they began to see another silhouette. Moving even closer, they saw Luke's hanging body, pale and bloody with clenched fists and pants pulled down to his ankles.

Aida looked up and saw her friend's lifeless corpse – bloody knuckles, fists tied with twine, pants down, eyes open and staring into the void. In the light flickering of the lantern, a greenish glow dancing on the ground, she saw the noose tightly wound around her friend's neck, tongue sticking out to one side with the fresh stench of death filling her nose. Aida began to experience tunnel vision, her mind and ears washing away hysterical screaming while her eyes focused on burn marks across the thighs and dismembered genitals. Her heart started beating harder and faster, the silence in her mind replaced with a blistering high-pitched ringing, slowly shifting from a nuisance in her ears to a pounding feeling in her head. She was disoriented and unable to move her body. The ringing became louder, the pain in her head greater, and her heartbeat fast enough to the point of dizziness and collapse, until a hand on her shoulder pulled her back to reality.

She started to hear her own screams. They rang loudly and echoed in her brain, which triggered a massive headache, unlike anything that she had ever felt. Then, she felt a shock in her body that radiated from her shoulder and locked the muscles in her arm.

She turned quickly to see what had happened, only to find BG's hand on her shoulder.

"Aida, we have to go." BG took his hand from Aida's shoulder and ran toward Lisa. Lisa had collapsed, curled up on the ground crying out "Why?" repeatedly into the darkness. Aida had turned back to Luke's dead body. Her vision tunneled into a single, thinly lit sight of Luke's face, swollen with his chin still tucked over a tight noose. She saw a mutilated shadow dangling through the darkness. Edmond was yelling incoherently and flailing his entire body. Marcus was stunned briefly, but then ran towards Luke's legs to lift him from the noose, hoping that there may be an ounce of life remaining. He found himself tangled in Luke's pants, yelling at the corpse to wake up. Aida started to feel dizzy and weightless, her mind and arms floating.

"We have to leave now!" yelled Marcus, as he dropped Luke's legs in exhaustion and desperation. Aida barely gained her composure.

They left their belongings in the cabin as they scrambled for the car. Lisa and Aida took the lead running side by side with Marcus and Edmond not far behind. Being the largest and least athletic of the group, BG was struggling to keep up.

"Keep running, babe!" called Lisa, as she tried to get BG to keep moving.

"Keep going! I'm right behind you!" yelled BG. "Bring the car back this way!"

Lisa picked up her pace to get into the car. Aida was continuing close behind her, when suddenly she tripped over a tree root. She rolled over another tree root and tumbled hard, injuring her ankle, which slowed down Marcus and Edmond when they stopped to pick her up.

At this point, Lisa was only a few feet away from the van.

Lisa cried out, "I'll come get you!" But as she started to open the door to the van, she heard a rustle of leaves and felt a quick gust of wind pass beside her. For a quick moment, she saw a face. The face of a tall, lanky, shadowy figure standing between her and her friends. The figure looked like the man they had seen earlier that day working on barrels, with his pale and cracked skin, long limbs, and stringy hair that looked like spider webs in the moonlight.

Lisa was frozen with fear as the shadow looked back at her. Her friends did not know what to do. They saw the shadow in the distance moving closer, and they could not figure out the next move. All they knew was that they would need to fight or run. Aida could only do one thing. She screamed as loud as she could.

"Lisa, go! Get help!"

Without hesitating, Lisa jumped into the van and turned the key, which had remained in the ignition while they were resting. The engine started running, and Lisa thrust her foot onto the gas pedal, peeling away in a cloud of dust.

"Why did she leave?" Edmond's voice shook from panic. He turned his wrath to Aida. "Why did you tell her to leave?"

"We need someone who can get help! Either we all die, or at least one of us survives. Don't you see?"

Marcus raised his voice and took charge of the situation. "No one is dying tonight." He straightened his back. "We need to get ready to fight." But before the group prepared themselves, the shadow sprinted toward them. Aida regained her footing and started running toward the large tree, along with BG, who was now ahead of Aida, since he fell so far behind. The shadow's footsteps gained quickly behind them with superhuman speed. Aida was injured, so she knew she was doomed. Marcus and Edmond had taken huge strides and blindly ran into the forest. With terror and burning air in her lungs, Aida almost gave up and accepted that this was probably the man responsible for what happened to Luke and that this could be the end. Suddenly, she felt a shove, which knocked her down. In the ensuing fall, she looked up to see the same figure's pale, lanky arms grab BG by the back of his shirt and lift him without any resistance, as if he were as light as a campfire marshmallow. Against the darkness of the night, BG looked like a ghost floating away into the forest.

Marcus and Edmond came back to regroup with Aida once the area fell silent.

"I thought something was about to happen," Edmond blurted confidently.

Marcus took control. "We need to get to safety until Lisa

comes back. Where's BG?"

BG was nowhere to be found.

"BG, aren't you back there? Where are you?" Marcus scrambled to find BG, thinking of it as a cruel joke.

"He's gone," she stated in a sullen, matter-of-fact tone.

" Aida, what do you mean he's gone?"

"Whatever that was, it took BG. Picked him up like he was nothing."

"Where did they go?

A loud scream bellowed from a long distance away. Marcus reacted, running in the direction of the scream. Edmond was too scared to move and curled into a ball on the ground.

Aida and Edmond were stuck - confused, disheveled, and terrified.

Aida's first instinct was to run, but she knew that outside of the Cottonwood Inn grounds, there were only miles of darkness around her. She screamed into the darkness to no avail. She stumbled back to the bed and breakfast to find safety, but the front door was locked. She ran to the nearest windows to see if she could find her way in. These windows were also locked. She wanted to check around the corners of the inn to see if there were any additional entrances, but the sides of the building were engulfed in darkness as well, and without knowing what may be around the other side, she stayed away. The way she saw it, she had only two choices - stay put and stay near the light next to the hanging corpse and make herself a target, or venture into the woods to find BG or Marcus. She chose the latter, forgetting that Edmond was still curled in the fetal position, whimpering quietly to himself.

She crept into the woods cautiously. She whispered softly but forcefully into the forest, trying to see if any of her friends were still close.

"Marcus? ... BG? ... "

She heard the crackling of every leaf and the motion of every branch against the bottom of her shoes. She had never felt her senses so heightened before, and the sensation made her more uneasy.

She started to see visions of creatures changing in front of her, interspersed with the terror-stricken faces of her still living friends, the swollen agony of her dead one, and the terrible, slender face of the man that caused this pain, all amplified against thin slivers of moonlight cracking in between tree branches and reflecting from small puddles.

After what felt live forever lurking through the woods, she felt a cold hand reach for her shoulder. She tried to scream, but another hand came from behind and covered her mouth. She began to fight erratically, scratching where her attacker's face and eyes should be. But the more she pulled and fought, the tighter and closer the hands would also pull. She thought this was the end for her, but the attacker quickly pulled her against his thin, waif-like body. He whispered aggressively in her ear.

"Stop it. You're going to get us both killed."

Aida started to calm down, her breathing still nervous but less labored. She recognized the voice.

"I'm going to take my hand away now. Don't yell."

The man behind her pulled his hands away slowly. Aida's body was shaking from the shock.

A faint light coming from behind her gently passed across the man's face. It was Edmond, who was also shaking and trying to remain calm.

"Aida, I'm freaking out right now. We need to find Marcus and BG."

Aida nodded, though Edmond was not able to clearly see what she was doing. Edmond was agitated.

"Aida, are you listening? I'm not doing well. I don't have my medicine, and I'm going to lose my mind. We need to get it together. We need to get back to the road and wait for someone to come by."

"We can't leave our friends. We can't leave Marcus and BG out here." Aida felt responsible. She had agreed to come back to this inn, and now her friends were all separated and victims of murder and abduction.

Edmond almost raised his voice but pulled himself back. "They're gone, Aida. They're done. We know we're okay, so we need to get out. We need to get out now."

"They went into the woods, and I don't think there's a way to get out over there."

"Aida, *please* listen to reason. This is no good. We have to go."

"I need to find them. You can leave me if you want to, but I'm going to go find them."

Aida started moving slowly into the woods again, but less carefully than before. She moved on instinct alone, without any plan on how she would move next, what she would do once she found her friends, or what she could do if trouble came for her.

Edmond wanted to continue his protest, but he knew two things. First, Aida is resolute and tenacious, so there was no talking her out of going. Second, although she tried to stay out of most petty issues, she would take charge if it meant keeping her friends safe. He begrudgingly stayed by her side.

Chapter 9

May 16, 2:17 AM

"Where is everyone?" Aida whispered into the darkness, hoping that Edmond was still nearby. Hoping that he would provide answers.

"Whatever that was that took BG away, it just snatched him and ran off. BG's a big guy, so I have no idea how that happened." Edmond moved carefully through the brush and broken branches. He realized that he needed to keep better pace if he did not want to be abandoned again.

"Edmond, keep up. We have to find them quickly. And where's Marcus?"

"Marcus ran some other way. I don't know if he tried to chase that guy." Edmond's voice wavered. "I'm really getting scared. I'm not sure I'm going to hold out much longer." It had been several hours since Edmond had taken his anxiety medication.

"Edmond, we need to stay calm. I'm sure they're going to be okay." She did not believe it, but Aida also knew that Edmond's anxiety would derail any chance of the group getting out of the forest.

"I'm really scared. I don't want to die out here."

"Me neither. You're not going to die out here."

The pair stumbled aimlessly through the forest for another fifteen minutes, looking for their lost friends.

Suddenly, they found a small sliver of light shining through the thick forest. The light glowed small, faint, and yellow, swaying back and forth in between the silhouettes of two trees. Aida reached her arm behind her to make sure that Edmond stopped to see what she was seeing.

"Hey, I think I see something. Edmond, can you see it?"

"A little. I'm not sure what that is."

"That's got to be something that can help. Maybe a place where we can hide or use a phone."

"I don't think so, Aida. It could be something even worse. Why would there be a phone out here? Can we just go back?"

"We have to try. I can't even tell you how to get back. This could be the only way."

"Fine. But you're walking ahead of me."

Aida reached back and grabbed Edmond's hand as the two of them moved slowly toward the source of the light. Against the distant stars that peeked through the tops of trees, the light could have easily blended into the night sky.

But as the two moved out of the darkness and closer to the source, they found that the light danced more, swaying back and forth with an effortless jiggle, and the glow began to take a reddish hue.

Edmond stared hard until he strained his eyes. "It looks like a fire."

They saw a sprawling grassy area, with the fire at the center, as they moved closer to the edge of the forest. It was faint, but it stood out against the darkness.

Branches began to clear from their feet, and they quieted their steps. They moved slowly into the circular clearing, with only a few loose twigs but no other obstructions. The clearing looked unnatural, as if created by human hands, with a perfect circle of dust around the fire. As they walked closer, the flame separated in half, exposing the shape of two burning torches, each one on either side of a large, thin tree. The tree had lots of thick branches, with a large object dangling loosely on a higher branch.

"What is that?"

"I don't know, Aida. Let's just leave."

"No, we have to see what that is."

"We really need to leave!" Edmond angrily exclaimed in his loudest whisper. "We can't keep going deeper. We need to get help!"

"Someone put this out here, which means there could be someone or something that can help us." Aida walked closer to the circle. The dancing flames cast light on a rope tied into many wooden posts, each of which was driven into the ground in a semicircle around the large tree. She walked around the tree to find any clue about the hanging object, as well as any signs of potential help.

"What does this lead up to?"

"Look, I've seen enough. I'm going back to see if I can flag someone down." As Edmond started retracing their path, he tripped over a rope.

"Ow, dammit!" screamed Edmond, as he landed on his knees and face.

"Shut up!"

"Shit, that really hurt," exclaimed Edmond, his voice sliding back into his aggressive whisper. He reeled from the pain. Aida ran over to help him up, but as she lifted him back on his feet, they heard a soft groan. Edmond's foot on the rope jarred the object above them, which they quickly realized was a person.

"Someone's up there," Aida blurted. "They sound hurt. We need to get them down."

"Aida, no. This looks like a set-up, and it smells funny around here. We need to go back and get real help."

"Listen, you do what you want. I'm going to help." Aida looked up at the tree. "Who are you? Are you okay?" Aida only received deep groans. "Are you okay?" she repeated, enunciating her words. She received more groans.

"I can't do it. I'm leaving." Edmond started to walk away, but he stopped when he looked at what Aida was trying to do.

"Fine! Why are you still here? Just leave." The ropes around the tree were interwoven, twisted around each other like a net and wrapped around the posts without being tied down. Because the ropes were large and thick, she was not able to just pull one of them over a post. Aida began searching and pulling on the ropes around the tree until she found a single knot tied at a post several feet away in the shadows of nearby trees. Using flickers of firelight, she jostled the rope, and she realized that the shifting of tension along the rope matched the motions of the person swaying above her.

She tugged the rope more vigorously and in rhythm, hoping to undo any knots or other fastening. Her hands slipped repeatedly, which caused intense bruising, but she pulled harder and harder with each tug.

"You can't be serious right now!" Edmond was louder than before. He forgot to remain as quiet as possible. Aida did not acknowledge him.

Just then, the rope loosened under Aida's hand. "I've almost got it."

She started tugging with both hands, which was tough because of the oil on the rope. She started feeling a tingle in her hands, but she persisted. After only a few moments, the rope loosened quickly and completely, whipping back and forth against itself as it untangled through its own weave. The sudden pull caused rope burns across Aida's palms and fingers. In her excitement, she did not even notice the pain until five seconds later. Neither of them noticed the small pieces of flint tied to the pole, nor did they notice the pieces of metal attached to the person who was dangling from the rope. The smell around them was strong now.

The scene looked like a meteor plummeting from the sky in a matter of seconds. The flames started from the falling person's feet and engulfed his entire body in a bright glow. The person let out a terrible scream, with agony in his voice and labored breathing in between the screams. A thin line of fire appeared from the body, travelling up the pole and coming back down the support ropes. The fire moved onto the posts on the ground, creating smaller fires around the body. The fire also ignited the oil on Aida's hands that transferred from the rope. The fire aggravated her rope burns, and she let out a yell while slamming her palms on the ground. Edmond stiffened in place, awed by what he was witnessing.

The body continued to squirm on the ground while it burned, the cries of agony becoming strained and more painful to bear. Aida pushed her hand deeper into the ground to cool her hands, then grabbed handfuls of soft dirt to throw onto the burning body. Her own burned hands made everything painful, but she kept on, not only for the sake of the burning victim, but also to keep the rest of the fire from spreading.

"Edmond! You have to help me!"

Edmond remained stiff. His anxiety had peaked, and it left him without control of his faculties.

"Ed!"

Edmond did not move.

Aida dug into the ground and tossed more and more dirt onto the rolling body. The person was writhing around, violently jerking and bound with rope and wires. He was crippled and unable to assist in his own rescue. Sparks and flickers of fire visually traced the outline of the large figure while the sound of his groans and rustles of foliage flooded Aida's ears. She dug faster and faster, tossing dirt faster and faster, screaming at Edmond louder and louder. He finally snapped out of his stupor to help Aida throw more dirt on the body. But by this time, the fire had been quelled.

They stepped back from the burning body in front of

them. The body smoldered, twitching while still bound in ropes and wires. Aida and Edmond tried to catch their breaths through the smoke and smell of fuel. Once the smoke cleared, they gasped in horror at the sight of the burnt, lifeless face of their friend BG.

Aida dove towards BG's lifeless body and quickly went to the ground to check his pulse. She screamed into his ear to wake him.

"BG? BG, wake up!" She shook his body. No response. She experienced the same hollow feeling from seeing Luke's body only moments ago. The fire around BG's body started fading away, and the stars in the sky began to disappear. Aida began to lose control in her muscles, and she could no longer feel the ground under her feet. But before she gave herself completely to that feeling, she felt a violent tug across her arm that nearly separated her shoulder. When she looked up, she found Edmond yanking her to her feet, pulling her back into the woods and away from the corpse of another friend.

Chapter 10

May 16, 2:48 AM

With the sound of crunching leaves from rushing feet and scratchy panting, Aida and Edmond had no time to get their bearings. They felt only the primal instinct to flee the open clearing and find refuge, moving swiftly and recklessly. They stayed away from the edge of the tree line, hoping to avoid being seen by the killer. Edmond tried to reach for Aida's hand in the rush, but Aida slapped Edmond's hand away as she ran into full dash. Edmond had forgotten how fast Aida could run, and though he felt vindicated in convincing Aida to finally run away, he was going to slow her down.

They sprinted down a steep hill near another small enclosure, nearly one thousand feet away from the edge of the clearing. The two stumbled over branches and roots as they moved erratically toward a small wooden toolshed sitting in a cleared area surrounded by tree stumps. The toolshed was simple, with a single door in the front, two small windows on each side of the door, and two small windows on either side of the shed, no bigger than the width of a human head. Corrugated iron laid across the shed's flat roof, and a small flower bed was set to the left of the door.

"Aida, we need to get in there." Edmond yelled as he pointed toward the shed.

"I don't think that's a good idea. We don't know if anyone is in there."

"Aida! Get in the shed!"

Aida realized that Edmond was right. He had been right about staying away from the fire, and he had been right to keep moving. Without any other options, Aida mustered her last bits of strength to sprint straight to the shed. But, with the additional momentum from running down the hill, she ran faster than normal and slammed her shoulder directly into the shed door. With a loud and harsh thud, the door swung open swiftly and a shooting pain ran straight into Aida's arm. She screamed out in agony as Edmond ran in after her, stopping short and pulling the door closed behind him. Edmond tried to lock the door, but the lock was broken. He opened and closed the door quickly, thinking that it would solve the problem. He tried to grab a brick that was on the ground, but the brick was not large enough to hold against the door. He quickly found a large stick, which was about the size and thickness of a large tree branch, and a large felling axe near the door of the cabin. He picked up both, one in each hand.

They quickly surveyed the cabin. With the smallest inkling of pale moonlight, they could see some of the items in the cabin. A flimsy wooden dinner chair with thin legs. A rocking chair with a tattered blanket laying messily on the seat. A dusty baby crib that had been left in disuse and disarray for many years. A pair of dark-colored work boots sitting in corner and dried with mud and leaves.

A small table near one of the windows with tiny wooden blocks and two tin coffee cups sitting on the tabletop, and several gardening tools strewn about the floor, including a rake and several hand tools. There were other smaller items that Aida and Edmond could feel through their shoes. They felt sharp, like stepping on jacks, but they did not focus too much on the pain in their feet. Rather, they worried about protecting themselves from an attack. They had seen what happened to Luke and BG, and they did not want to be the next victims.

"What are we going to do?" whispered Aida.

"I don't know." Edmond spat words hurriedly in between heavy breaths. "We need to find something to protect ourselves."

"Okay, what are we going to use?"

Edmond frantically looked around through the dark.

"Grab the brick." He pointed down to the brick that he just moved. "We can get the drop on anyone if they try to come in."

Aida bent down and grabbed the brick, holding it tightly in her right hand. She prepared to deal severe damage to anyone that threatened them. Edmond decided that if they were going to be attacked, he wanted to end the man for good. He held the axe with one hand and moved the stick away from the door.

"I'm gonna open the door before he rams through. If things go crazy, I'm gonna swing the axe." Aida nodded quickly and prepared herself for an ambush.

They waited for just a few minutes, though it felt like hours to them. Aida moved into a low, seated catcher's position directly across the cabin door, while Edmond continued to look through the window to the right of the door. They were tired from the running, and it was so late in the evening that they could barely keep their eyes open. Suddenly, Edmond saw a tall silhouette appear from the woods, rustling through bushes and running through tree branches at a lightning pace.

"Aida, he's coming. Get ready."

She tightened her grip around the brick. She held it so tight that she did not notice the small droplets of blood trickling from the hand. She could only hear the quick, pulsing beat of her heart. She could not see the running figure, only the door. She felt herself sliding back into her heightened state, except instead of being frozen by terror, her body felt fluid and poised to attack.

Edmond positioned his body away from the moonlight coming through the window, still managing to see the figure running toward the cabin growing ever closer and larger. He tried to steady the axe with both hands with no success. His normal anxiety levels would have caused his hands to shake the axe mildly, but in a dangerous situation, he rattled the blade as if controlled by an angry spirit. The blade kept moving against the light, creating a faint shine that moved back and forth across Aida's face. She remained unaware, staring directly at the door for her chance to move. All the while, the figure moved closer and louder.

"I'm going to swing. You hit him with the brick."

"Are we going to kill him?"

"I don't want to, but what choice do we have? He's coming for us." In truth, Edmond was unsure of what he really wanted to do. He had never gotten into a fist fight, let alone thought of killing anyone, but he had never been in a situation where he could be murdered. Edmond decided that he was not going to let this man get him. He dropped the stick and gripped the axe.

The footsteps moved faster and became louder as the shadow took the shape of a man, grunting hoarsely and flailing his arms and legs hysterically.

"Get ready." Edmond tightened his grip around the axe

handle and pulled it back to swing.

"Okay." Aida pulled the brick back, preparing for a throw.

The figure was close. The breathing became heavier and guttural. Suddenly, he was upon the door. Edmond had been tracking his movements since he first saw him, and now was ready to strike. The figure ran straight for the door, lowering himself to ram it open.

Edmond called out. "Now."

Edmond flung the door open before the man could push it, and he swung the axe handle with all his strength. Edmond had expected recoil from the impact of the axe handle, but his shaky grip made the axe slip further up his hands, causing the axe blade to drop further as he swung. This caused the blade to bury deep into the mysterious man. The figure's legs lifted from under him, as if he slipped cartoonishly on a banana peel.

Aida launched the brick less than a second after Edmond's swing, causing the brick to fly out of her hand and through the doorway onto a tree stump outside. The brick shattered into pieces, and the cracking sound pierced through the trees surrounding the cabin. Edmond and Aida were shocked when they saw the axe standing straight up, firmly planted into the figure's chest. They were more shocked when they realized that the figure they had just attacked was not the man who had been stalking them all night, but their friend Marcus, who had found the cabin to seek the same refuge.

"Holy shit!" screamed Edmond. "Why? Why?" He immediately became hysterical, screaming in between saying "no" to himself repeatedly while pacing back and forth. Aida tried to remove the axe, which only caused more blood to spew forth. She quickly realized that there would be no way to save him. She looked at Marcus's face, staring blankly at the ceiling, the charming energy and beautiful soul fading from Marcus's face. She dropped to the ground, losing control of her muscles, covered in tears and sweat, as she watched her closest friend dying before her.

Marcus stretched his neck slightly, fixing his lips to say his final words. Aida leaned near his face to hear him.

"Aida… I saw him…" He hesitated as he choked on fluids. Aida leaned in closer to keep him from struggling.

"Aida, he wasn't coming for me." His eyes slowly closed, and his body began to twitch.

Edmond screamed out in agony. "Shit!" He jumped toward the door and was met with a punch to the face, knocking him unconscious.

Aida looked up fast enough to see the mysterious man, dressed in dark clothing, showing only his stringy hair and thin, jagged facial features. She tried to push through him and escape, but she felt her body turn quickly as she felt his emaciated arms wrap around her neck, putting her in a chokehold until she passed out.

Chapter 11

May 16, 5:44 AM

Aida awakened groggy with a throbbing headache, and her vision was blurry. Her headache began to subside and her vision returned. She realized she was lying on the floor of a different cabin, one that was large and filled with workbenches and tools. She saw everything through flickers from soft lanterns sitting on tables. The air smelled of burning oil, like a stronger version of what she smelled around BG earlier in the night. It was noxious, like the diesel fuel from the trucks that would drive past her neighborhood. Still in a daze, she tried to get up from her knees but was stopped by chains weighing down her arms and chest. She started to sob quietly. She saw the visions of her friends dying - Luke hanging, BG burning, Marcus bleeding - and she knew that she would be next. She hung her head and wept as the chains rattled against her body.

After thirty-five minutes, both her vision and her brain fully cleared. *This is the barrel maker's cabin*, she thought. She hoped to find something that would help her escape. She saw small tools on the benches, but those were too far away for her to reach. There were other larger, more exotic tools, including those she saw near his work area the day before, but she did not know how to use them and was worried that she might hurt herself more if she tried.

She pulled herself up to her knees and leaned forward to see how far the chains would go. *About six inches, not very far.* The pain still throbbed in her ankles and wrist. She was tethered to a horse's hitching rail. There were strange coins and weird paper money strewn across tables and peppered along the floor, both of which had rotted and faded from years of neglect.

She heard the pounding of a hammer against solid wood from outside, followed by heavy footsteps dragging a large object against the dusty ground. The footsteps stopped shortly after, ending with a sudden thud against squeaking metal. Aida presumed that whatever the barrel maker was dragging, he just lifted into something big, like a machine. Hearing the ominous sound from just outside, it confirmed that her time was over. She quieted her sobbing and relaxed her muscles from top to bottom. She remained terrified, but she would not give her captor the satisfaction of hearing her scream.

As she resigned to her fate, the front door opened slowly and the barrel maker walked in. He was wearing a large and tattered charcoal gray coat, a frayed large-brimmed hat, black pants, and black boots with small holes along the sides that showed his ghostly, ashen feet. He had a small fabric of lace around his left wrist, which contrasted against the thick, black leather gloves that gave a dreadful squeak as he moved his fingers around his large hammer.

Aida could not see his face through the stringy, oily hair with red flecks that danced across the man's face, like tiny embers against black threads.

The man walked over to a work bench across from Aida, where he put down a stack of the same unusual coins that she saw around the cabin. The man said nothing to Aida. He laid his hammer on the table and wiped his forehead. She began to goad him.

"I want to go home."

He remained silent while sharpening a large hunting knife. Aida raised her voice.

"Are you going to do something? Or are you going to let me go?" She could feel herself becoming more agitated. Her eyes welled up with tears, but she tried to remain composed.

He said nothing.

"Please! Just let me go!" She could no longer hold back. Her tears flowed harder than before, and she pulled harder against her chains. The violent and erratic rattling of metal did not faze her captor, who continued his work unbothered. He did not flinch for a moment, even as she struggled. Her wrists began to scrape and bleed against the shackles. Her body felt weaker and weaker as she sank lower and lower. Standing became harder as she struggled more.

The barrel maker finished sharpening his blade and turned slowly towards her. His face was covered by his hat and his stringy strands of hair, but she could still see his translucent skin and sunken cheeks. His mouth opened slightly, showing only a few rotten teeth and no sign of a tongue. His face showed no emotion other than murderous intent in his eyes.

Aida started seeing memories of her family. She saw her mother and father, her three sisters joking together in the living room, her aunt and uncle in the house for holidays. She saw the faces of her friends that died that night - Luke, BG, Marcus. She saw Edmond's fear when he killed Marcus. She saw Lisa's terrified look before she jumped in the van and drove away. She thought about her future, and her reasons to live. She could not accept this. She yelled for someone to come save her, for someone to break through the door and fight off the man. She yelled for Edmond. She cried out to Lisa, hoping that she would come back for them just in time.

The man moved closer to her, lifting the knife to waist level. She saw remnants of dried blood near the bottom of the blade and on the top of the handle, and there was the small piece of delicate lace tied around his wrist. He stretched his hand out and positioned the blade of the knife against her abdomen, ready to sink it in. In a panic, she blurted out Marcus's last words, hoping that it could save her at the last moment.

"You weren't coming for me!"

He cocked his head slowly to one side and loosened his grip around the knife's handle. He stood motionless for ten seconds. Aida flinched, thinking that he was preparing to end it. She kept her eyes shut, hoping to be spared the last sight of his face before her death. He pulled his hair away from his face to get a better look at her.

She opened her eyes to see him standing straight up and two feet in front of her, a pair of gray sullen eyes, absent of any humanity and darkened by an unknown force that barely distinguished the irises from the whites. His skin was dry as dust and flaked just the same. A large W-shaped vein throbbed in his forehead, and his nose was sharp and disfigured. Without moving the position of his knife, he quickly thrust his face forward closer to her face. This caused Aida to flinch again, this time with a small whimper as she continued shaking. The man cocked his head slightly to the other side as he looked at Aida. He studied her features, moving his eyes back and forth across her mouth, her ears, her nose. She shivered as she felt his shallow, cold breath across her face. She opened her eyes again, with his face only inches away. He stared directly into her eyes. She saw into him, deep into his soul, and all she saw was an empty void, without any warmth or decency.

He slowly moved away from her and put the hunting knife back in its belt holster. He opened his mouth slightly and gave a small grunt through her heavy breathing.

"Hmm…" The sound was deep and gurgling, like his lungs were filled with fluid.

He opened his long gray coat and drew a large hatchet from one of the pockets inside his coat. As a reflex, Aida screamed in panic and turned her head as the man brought the hatchet in the air. With a quick motion, he brought the blade down. Except, the blade did not go into her. Rather, it cut straight through the chains holding her arms together.

Her arms dropped to the ground like lead bars, and the force caused her to fall forward on her knees. As she felt the pain of her knees hitting the hard, wooden floor, the man broke the chains near her waist and legs with the hatchet. He then pulled forward on the chains in between her wrists, which slid Aida in a prone position. He cut those chains as well. The last chains fell to the ground, and the sound reverberated through the cabin. Aida was confused, relieved, and mad, all of which poured out of her in a series of gasps, crying, and hyperventilation. The man stood up, put the hatchet back in his coat pocket, and walked out of the cabin, leaving Aida to compose herself.

Aida was even more confused than before, but she felt like she was given a second chance. While the pain from the weight of her chains dissipated, the weight on her mind and her lungs was slower to go away. She rubbed her extremities to make sure that her blood was moving, pushing the blood through the muscles in her arms and legs and into her fingers and toes. She rubbed her ankles and wrists gently to check for irritation or cuts from her shackles, then she picked herself up from the floor. She glanced around the room once more to make sure she was safe from the man, or any others who might be supporting him. There was no sign of anyone else nearby. She slowly walked toward the exit door, past the tools, and the benches, and the coins and paper bills, and the chains and ropes that dangled around the cabin. She turned the squeaky doorknob, and as she took a step through the doorway, she tripped over a branch and stumbled outside.

She fell to the ground hard on her stomach, the pain jolting into her organs. She rolled onto her back to take the pressure away from her gut and looked up to the sky. She laid briefly, coughing through the pain, briefing taking in a view of the moonlight and stars dancing in between dust particles.

As her eyes adjusted to the darkness, she faintly saw a red short-bed pickup truck sitting a short distance away from the door. The bed of the truck was open with a large wooden barrel tied loosely with ropes. Not wanting to miss her chance to escape, Aida stood up and ran to the truck.

Not only was the door open, but the keys were also sitting in the driver's seat. Aida was relieved but exhausted from the sprint. For however long she was chained in the cabin, it had caused her muscles to stiffen, and her fall just outside the cabin had really knocked the wind out of her. She grabbed the keys, jumped in the car, and turned the key in the ignition. She tried to drive away immediately, but the truck's seat was too far back, and she began to panic. She flailed her right foot, hoping to find the pedals before the barrel maker changed his mind. The tunnel vision that she felt earlier started to appear again. Suddenly, instinct took over. Her left arm found a lever below the seat, which she pulled quickly. The driver's seat suddenly slid forward, and after a few moments, the adrenaline coursing through her veins took over. She shifted the car into the driving position and pushed her foot hard onto the gas pedal.

The car bumped over the dusty ground as Aida swerved around shadowy structures along both sides of the exit. Once she escaped the clearing, she drove past the front entrance of the Cottonwood Inn, nearly smashing into the fragile wooden sign. She did not understand how she survived her impending demise, but through her teary, labored breathing, she was just glad to escape. Aida kept maneuvering through the dark highway, but she was partially distracted by the barrel in the cab of the truck.

The road felt as if it was slowly fading away, leaving only a rock-filled deathtrap that rattled the truck in every direction possible. The dust cloud formed by Aida's erratic driving entered the truck and covered the windshield and side windows with a thin layer that made seeing the road difficult. The banging of metal and wood became more intense. Something about that sound began to drive her crazy, as if the sound originated in her mind. The slamming of the barrel against the walls of the truck bed became louder and louder in Aida's ears, and her heart raced faster and faster with each thud. Sweat poured into her eyes, causing her to briefly lose control of the car and drift near the edge of the road. Fearing that she would drive off the road, she jerked the steering wheel suddenly, which forced the door lock of the truck bed to dislodge and sent the barrel out of the truck's cabin crashing onto the street against the dim moonlight.

Aida tried to compensate for pulling the steering wheel so quickly, but her second attempt at pulling the wheel back proved to be too much, and the truck tipped over and slammed onto the road, passenger side down. Everything around her felt silent, as her arms and legs hung across the right side of her body toward the street. She was too tired to scream from the pain, and she did not have the strength to moan or cry. The night was ending, and Aida began to lose consciousness. Against the light of the breaking dawn, she saw the faint flashing of red and blue lights against the broken car mirrors.

She woke up to police officers, sheriff's deputies, and firefighters lifting her out of the truck. Aida could hear the faint voice of her friend Lisa through the barking of orders among the officers and deputies. She was giving a statement to a sergeant of the Lorro Police Department. Lisa drove directly to the police station in Lorro and returned with help.

Aida felt her body being placed on the gurney, and a sheriff's deputy approached her to take her statement. She mumbled to the deputy about her friends still missing in the woods and that she was looking for them before she took the car. She began sobbing quietly while medical staff lifted her into an ambulance and checked her vital signs and bones for breakage. Before the medical staff could warn anyone, Aida felt her blood pressure increasing and her heart racing, and the sweat on her forehead dripping down her face. She became lightheaded from the intensity.

The deputy put away her notepad and cursed to herself under her breath. Aida passed out.

Chapter 12

May 16, 12:47 PM

When Aida woke up several hours later, she was handcuffed and laying on a gurney at the Lorro City Hospital. Her vision was blurry but coming into focus over time, and her body ached all over. Over several hours, nurses entered and exited, providing food, cold packs, water, and comfort. Her parents remained outside the room for most of her time there, as did the patrol officer stationed outside of her room door. Her mother occasionally stood up to get water from the water fountain. Her father quietly sat in the hallway, staring blankly at the hospital walls. Marcus's father, unaware of what exactly happened, came to the hospital to visit Aida for answers, but Aida had fallen asleep before he was able to speak to her. The patrol officer outside of her door stated that even if she were awake, he had orders to keep any visitors away except for hospital staff, at least until she was discharged. Aida's mother took Marcus's father to the cafeteria to get coffee. Aida's father scowled at both of them, then turned away to stare at a different wall. Her father never liked Marcus's, which Aida attributed to Marcus's father being more prominent and successful.

When she finally woke up later that evening, Aida gave

her statement to the police about the trip to Minstrel Lake.

She told them about the drinking and the partying, and about the emergency when Luke fell ill. She told them about Esther and Dottie at the Cottonwood Inn, the lanky barrel maker in dark clothing that killed her friends, the large tree with the red soil where Luke hung, the tree in the clearing where BG burned, the tool shed where Marcus was killed, and the workshop that she ultimately escaped. The police conducted a thorough search of the area around Route 87. They found Luke's mangled body hanging from the large cottonwood tree. They found BG's burned corpse on the ground in the clearing in the woods, as well as a charred copy of his comic book. There were no restraints or anything to suggest how he was set on fire, and the body reeked of kerosene oil. They found the small shed where the body of Marcus laid on the rotted floor, the axe still in his chest with dried blood around the blade and insects crawling around the wound. They found Edmond's body on the side of Route 87, with holes punctured throughout his body. They also found wooden pieces of a barrel, several of which had large nails hammered into them. Based on how the state examiners had reassembled the barrel for evidence, the nails were hammered into the barrel while Edmond was trapped inside, stabbing and prodding him as the barrel rolled and swayed.

What the investigators did not find was the Cottonwood

Inn, or any trace of Esther, Dottie, and the unknown barrel maker. No clothing, no food, no newspapers or bear claws or jars filled with different substances. Nothing.

Lisa did not provide many additional details. She corroborated everything that Aida reported to the authorities, confirming that there was a lanky man terrorizing them kept Aida from being the primary suspect. She hoped that once she provided her statement, she would finally get to see BG. The authorities later informed her that BG was found dead.

She blamed Aida. She knew that Aida did not kill their friends or set them up to be killed. She knew that even if she did want to kill them, even if deep inside she harbored enough resentment to desire murder, she would not be physically or emotionally capable of doing what she saw that night or coordinating such an attack. But reason and logic failed her. Aida had told them they had to leave their camp at Minstrel Lake, and in Lisa's mind, if they had not left that night, they would still be alive. Lisa felt the weight of everything on her spirit. She wanted BG to still be alive. She wanted to stop feeling the pain, and she had nowhere to channel those feelings. Graduation was approaching the following Saturday. She needed to keep herself together.

News of what happened during senior weekend at the lake had spread through the town, so she kept herself composed long enough to get away and never see anyone else again. She cut off all communication with Aida, without acknowledging what had happened to them or any of Aida's feelings. Aida was hurt when she realized that Lisa was ignoring her calls.

She had lost every one of her closest friends, and now she was losing the only person still alive that could understand how she was feeling. Aida was crushed. Lisa no longer cared.

The state police were brought in to assist in the investigation, and their agency needed time to sort out the facts. Plus, they wanted the students at Lorro High School to celebrate their accomplishments and did not want the tragedy to hang over their heads more than it already was, though that did little to ease the feelings of the students and school administration alike. A memorial was hastily prepared in the dead students' honor, with special awards, a presentation of their contributions to the school, and nearly ten minutes of standing ovation.

Lisa and Aida did not attend.

The ensuing media storm was relentless. For such a small, sleepy town, what began was the circus of rumors, half-truths, and conspiracy theories. Aida provided a detailed account of the entire evening to the authorities on multiple occasions, but only a few facts of the case were officially released to the public - the names of the victims, the general area on Route 87, the fact that it occurred during the big weekend visit to Minstrel Lake, and a few credible theories of the crime. They kept specific details out of the news for two reasons. First, the police department did not want to harm the community with the gory details. The death of such young people already shook the town to its core, and they did not want to amplify the pain and mourning.

Second, they were not entirely convinced that Aida was telling the truth. There was nothing in Aida's demeanor or physical stature that indicated she was capable of the crimes, but the idea that some outside person could be responsible for so many murders in the same general geographic area without leaving any trace of themselves was far-fetched.

The police were inundated with questions on how and why the killings happened. They could not provide the public with a plausible story, no matter how much coordination there was among the different agencies. Lisa confirmed Aida's story to a point, but Aida was the only person claiming to have witnessed everything after that. Aida survived, which made her the primary suspect in the eyes of the public.

They interviewed classmates, teachers, her coaches, and nothing indicated that she was violent in any way. Investigators considered that she worked with a partner, but wanting to kill her closest friends, even wanting to kill Luke, was a stretch beyond their imagination. Other people had more elaborate theories – a jilted lover gone mad, an estranged business partner of one of their parents exacting revenge, a drifter or a desperate escaped prisoner, anarchists, killer clowns. In the more fringe areas of the Lorro community, there was talk of zombies, ghosts, and aliens.

No one took these theories seriously, and the Lorro police chief announced that any police officers making suggestions or public statements about supernatural beings or baseless theories would be reprimanded and quickly dismissed from the case.

After several months on the case, the state police announced that the case would be continued at a limited capacity, due to other priorities and a lack of further facts beyond their exhaustive search. Followers of the unsolved case of the "Lorro Four" pushed more sinister ideas. For them, intervention from the federal government, shadowy secret societies, and international financial institutions had all been responsible for the murders, a way to distract the public while creating a new order or conducting illicit scientific experiments.

The talk of foul play inspired several people to travel to Georgia to find the scene of the crimes and search for treasure or other clues, hoping to find out where the cover-up occurred. The endless newcomers, with their, shovels and metal detectors, had interfered with the ongoing investigation and those that came to pay their respects to the dead. This forced the Governor to issue a plea for peace and respect for the Lorro citizens. Most complied and some still came, but eventually the fiasco was forgotten by all but only the few ardent enthusiasts.

Aida stayed in Georgia. The trauma kept her in the house and away from any activity for several years - no college, no running, no friends, nothing.

The university that accepted Aida offered her unlimited deferment for her admittance, meaning that she could start her studies at any time that that she chose once she became well. In the meantime, her family became part of a relentless and expanding media cycle. Over a few years, several networks started searching for her and her family over the internet, as well as the families of the victims. National evening news shows wanted her on live television to discuss what she saw and how she thought the murders really happened. She was not interested.

The producers of *A Current Affair* were the first to knock on her door. They wanted to dig into some of the more chilling allegations that were whispered around the country. National television and radio networks commented on the story relentlessly, hoping to keep eyes glued to the television and ears glued to the airwaves. The story ginned up interest in otherwise lackluster coverage, at least until the next juicy crime took over the attention of the masses. With the proliferation of new twenty-four hours networks, commentators eventually sunk their teeth into the story. The cable news networks eventually made their way to the story, taking interviews with friends and family of the slain teens and focusing heavily on Aida. Aida was framed as both sympathetic and devilish, a young girl with a promising future in academics and athletics whose questionable involvement in one of the most brutal killings in Georgia's history derailed everything that was important to her and her family.

Reporters were still skeptical about what part she played, and pundits talked ad nauseum about the appropriateness of parading her around in the national spotlight. The irony of these public discussions was lost on them.

Aida did not want any of this, but the stress took a toll on her family's livelihood. Her father's job as an accountant was under threat, as he was the father of "that girl who killed her friends." No one felt any confidence in a man that would "raise such a girl." Her mother had been shunned by her friends in Lorro for the same reason.

The shame was too great, so Aida dragged herself out of her self-imposed exile once in a while for an interview to get paid. It helped her family pay bills and purchase necessities. She never wanted any of this, but it was the only option they had for any security and peace.

Aida fell into a mental health crisis in the years after graduation. With the help of her family and a few acquaintances from school, she gathered the strength to check into a psychiatric clinic, where she gained the help she desperately needed - regular exercise, medication, counseling, and group therapy. She continued to have flashbacks and nightmares, but she learned to manage during her time at the clinic. She did not make many new friends while she was in therapy. Most of the people at the facility were much older, with not much else to bring them together. She wanted to focus on mental and emotional stability, as well as get herself into physical shape for the day when she could safely leave and return to competitive running.

Still, she had a long road ahead of her. She kept having flashbacks of that night, picturing herself as both the killer and the killed. She found herself inside the man's body, staring at her own body in chains. She felt herself dangling in the air, on fire, pain in her chest and body full of holes. She went to sleep every night overcome with anxiety, and she woke up every morning breathless and drenched in sweat.

Eventually the hospital discharged her, but she knew she would not find peace for a long time. She kept herself covered and avoided gatherings, afraid that someone would recognize her and harass her. She knew about the sick torture junkies that wanted her to relive her pain publicly for their amusement. Aida was not going to let the fear win. She read at least one book a week, ran at least twice a week, took her medicine every day, and spoke with counselors frequently. Over time, she increased her reading and running and decreased her medications. As time further passed, she relied less and less on interventions, but her doctors told her that she would still need medication for the rest of her life, even if they were infrequent. The flashbacks and nightmares were not stopping, but she learned to manage.

Once Aida found normalcy, she began to take classes at a local community college. She had hoped to go back to Lorro before courses started, but she had spent so much time away and feared that returning home too soon would lead to a relapse.

She had taken one or two classes each semester for six years, ranging from architecture and mathematics to philosophy and history - her favorite subject. In every semester, she felt overly stressed with the workload and expended too much mental energy to focus. The only semester where she managed her coursework in a healthy way was the semester where she enrolled in multiple history courses.

Starting in her fifth year of taking classes, she included an additional history course each semester, as well as a creative writing course. She enjoyed the balance of mental flexing and solitude that creative writing and historical research provided. She found her calling, and with the chance to take full semesters, she pursued a history degree with a minor in creative writing. Her interest was so strong that she mustered the courage to leave Georgia for a doctorate.

Aida found purpose in her schoolwork, and with the help of her graduate school advisor and colleagues, regular therapy, and medication, she remained calm and productive, though she still had night terrors. Outside of her coursework and an occasional outing with her classmates, most of her interactions were with doctors and nurses. As far as she was concerned, there was no one that could understand what she had been through, no one that could have seen the horror and felt the terror. But she knew the alternative would be much worse. For her, what was scarier than a person who did not understand her, was a person that did understand her.

Every day was still a struggle. Some days were better, some were worse. After she graduated with her doctorate, she became a shut-in, leaving only occasionally to see the outside the world. She watched both of her younger sisters graduate from high school. She saw her older sister graduate from veterinary school. She joined them again with their mother at their father's funeral.

She still received interview requests about the "Lorro Four." By this time, the media had given it a new name, "The Massacre at Minstrel Lake." She rebuffed all of the requests. Her mother found work as an office clerk in Lorro, and her sisters contributed more financially to the household as they got older. Other than those from her family, she stopped picking up phone calls. As the internet emerged as the primary communication vehicle, she carefully screened her email and chat messages. When she found work in academia, she always ran into students that were familiar with the case. Some showed comfort and concern, some showed interest for scientific or historical reasons, some were unusually excited about the gory details. Aida, known as Dr. Barnett to her students, was not interested in indulging any of these impulses. She eventually left teaching and decided to focus exclusively on research.

After many years away, Dr. Barnett found herself back in Georgia. She had finished her thesis on migration trends and economic foundations of the southern United States, which later garnered her a few citations in obscure academic journals and a few private guest talks. A small liberal arts school in Georgia had an opening for a researcher, focusing on her specialty. She was hesitant to return to her home state, but she missed her family and wanted to be closer to them. Her sisters were all married. Aida suspected they got married so young in order to change their name and separate themselves from their family. Despite her now-strained relationships with them, she looked forward to seeing her nieces and nephews at some point. With a long interview process and some key recommendations, Aida found herself in a small town forty-five miles away from Lorro, doing the work that she loved, close enough to loved ones but far enough away to not be constantly reminded of her trauma.

Chapter 13

March 20, 2007, 7:14 PM

Dr. Barnett spent most of her days in a library, reading old documents and manuscripts, reviewing student essays and papers, and assisting graduate students on the intricacies of historical analysis and the importance of understanding the finer details. When she was not in the basement of a library or conducting office hours, Aida would read at home while listening to jazz or American folk music. Each night for her ended around eight thirty in the evening with warm tea and a review of the day. She tried to avoid any type of romance or social outings, especially anything outside at night. She missed a lot of events - concerts, events with guest lecturers, the wedding receptions for her younger sisters. Being around people always felt like a risk to her well-being, so she did her best to reduce time with others.

One evening, Aida went into a private collection, deep within the Harrison Berry Memorial Library, to review older documents related to the Reconstruction period. She was due to write a comparative study on post-Civil War sentiment toward the enslaved people of Georgia and surrounding states as it compared with other movements across the world. She was to complete the work in two years, along with companion pieces written for the university every three months after that.

The students were on their spring break, and while she would normally take the week to catch up on grading student papers or planning new projects, this year's break provided Aida a rare opportunity to explore the subjects that she loved. She poured over old manuscripts, large encyclopedic texts, pamphlets, brochures, newspapers, anything that would organize her thoughts before she reached out to any colleagues with other insights. For the first few days of the break, she heard only the sound of her own footsteps and movement of pages echoing through halls. It was glorious.

But on the Thursday of that spring break, another woman was already sitting at one of the tables in the collection room when Aida walked in, reading from a large, aged book.

She was incredibly beautiful, sitting with straight posture in a light blue dress with long sleeves and white buttons that trailed all the way up to a frilly white collar. Her hair was pulled back into a single ponytail, showing a puff of hair behind her pleasant brown face, and a small pair of reading glasses gently stayed near the tip of her nose as she flipped through pages. Aida was startled. She was not aware of anyone else in the history department with access to that collection that remained on campus for the break. She had not even seen this woman on campus before.

"Oh, hello," Aida whispered as she walked in the room.

The young lady looked up from the book, never breaking her perfect posture. "Hello there." She cracked a smile as she spoke.

Aida stood in the doorway. "I didn't realize anyone else was around this week."

"Oh, I come through here from time to time." She paused briefly while Aida walked further into the room. "I believe I've seen you once before."

"Really?" Aida began to put her items on a chair at another table. "I don't remember seeing you around here."

"Hmm, interesting. Well, I hope you remember me if you see me again after today."

Aida felt a little uneasy about this woman. How had she seen Aida without herself noticing this lady? She was usually good at paying attention to her surroundings, though there were moments where she would lose herself in thought and tune out the world when she was engulfed in her study. She stated calmly, "I hope so, too."

Aida sat down at her table and took out her notepad. She spread her papers across the table, ordering everything in neat piles and writing notes on each pile to organize her thoughts. She wrote down her agenda for accomplishing her work, as well as a brief list of where she could find potential sources for review. She also took out a cinnamon roll, a bottle of water, and a small bottle of anxiety medication. In the middle of her organizing ritual, she took two bites of her roll, tossed a pill into her mouth, and chased the food and medication with her water.

The young woman took notice. "What are you taking?"

"My anxiety medication."

"Have you always taken it?"

"No, I haven't." Aida was increasingly annoyed. No one had ever asked about her medical regime, and she tried to keep that part of her life separate from others. Still, she did not feel uncomfortable about sharing information with this woman, which, in a way, made her uncomfortable about how comfortable she was. "I've been through some things."

"I can understand. I was very broken up after my mother passing away many years ago."

"Really? I lost my father a few years ago. I was already dealing with a lot in my life, and his passing made things even harder for a while. Was your father around in your life?"

The young lady sighed. "Oh no, he died before my mother did. He was murdered."

Aida was taken aback. "Oh no! That's awful. I'm so sorry that happened. I hope they got the guy."

"*Guys*, actually. I was a little girl when they got my dad. Unfortunately, there wasn't anything we could do to stop them. We just had to continue living our lives."

"There wasn't a trial of some sort? Why weren't they able to catch them?"

The woman took a deep breath and looked off into the distance, remembering some long-lost pain that she wanted to share with someone else.

"You know, it's a funny thing. You think that people would have figured out how to get along by then. And if they didn't, you'd think they would know how to try and make the wrong things right.

And if not that, then at least leave each other be, so that we could just exist without all the trouble. Then you live where I lived, and see what I saw, and suddenly, that way of thinking isn't true anymore. I learned that when I was really young, after my father died. I learned that when my mother had to keep living near the man that was responsible for my father's death." She began to tear up. "And when I asked her why we had to live like that, around killers and those who gave the killers power, she told me that sometimes, 'that's just how it had to be if you wanted to live another day. But, one day, the people that put you in danger, and kept you from really shining, they would see their time come.' And when they did, there was no one there to give them release. No one there to tell them that they lived a good life. No one to say that they were genuinely good people. And the eternal pain of living in Hell without absolution was more intense than any pleasure that may have come for you in this life. So, I put on a brave face and smiled, and dealt with all that anger and hurt, until the day my father's killer was killed himself. And he didn't get any relief from what he did, and that gave me all the joy that I needed. It didn't bring my father back, but I felt some real joy that day." The woman flipped the page back to the beginning of the chapter she was reading. "It's why I like to come down here and read this book."

Aida hesitated, chilled by the woman's words. "I… I don't understand."

"Mmm…" The young woman gently nodded her head and changed the subject. "Ma'am, do you have any regrets in life?"

Aida looked down and sighed. "Several."

The woman nodded gently again. "I don't think there are a lot of truly evil people in the world, but they do exist. Despicable, horrible, ungodly people. Something happened to them a long time ago, before they became so evil, that they had no control over and don't even know how to fix. But those people do not deserve our love. Then there are those that are not evil, but they are just mean. Not very nice, and don't have any desire to learn or be better. They won't burn in the next life, but they will suffer here. Then, there are some that are generally nice, but they will be affected by the ones that are mean, and they'll suffer. Then some will become overwhelmed and pushed to insanity, and they will suffer, and they will make their loved ones suffer. They can be dangerous because they become a threat to themselves and their loved ones." She paused briefly, then continued.

"And sometimes, there are some really good people, but they're scared. They will suffer in a different way. They will see those that suffer around them, and no matter how much they want to help, they can't. They have the means and the privilege and the good fortune to get through the suffering, and they will come out of their trials feeling guilty for not being able to help. Those people will suffer the worst, but they will be alive." She paused again, letting her words linger in the air.

"The things that I read down here remind me of that life. That you must pay attention to the ugliness of the world. It reminds me of what we came from and where we need to go." She stood up from her seat and walked toward the stacks. "We have a long struggle ahead, and as my mother always said about getting justice, 'We never retire. The struggle continues.'"

Those words rang in Aida's ears. Those were the same words that the older woman Esther said to her, a day before her friends took their trip from Lorro to Minstrel Lake all those years ago. Aida hesitated, then she slowly stood up to walk over to the woman, indignant but fearful.

"Ma'am, who are you?"

The woman kept walking toward the stacks, disappearing behind one of the taller shelves. Aida saw only the flip of a bright orange ribbon swing from her large, beautiful puff of brown curly hair and down her back. As Aida walked toward the shelves, she turned the corner to see no one, only an empty aisle filled with books on either side.

She walked back to the table where the woman was sitting to see the large book closed, a book she had never seen before in the collections. The title of the book was *Curious Legends and Unbelievable Myths*. There was a small piece of paper, wedged in the pages as a bookmark. She opened the book to where the bookmark was and pulled the small piece of paper out. It was a picture of an owl, hand drawn by a child and torn from another piece of paper.

She recognized it. It was the same owl that she saw on the picture that Dorothy gave to her mother Esther all those years ago. She sat down in the woman's vacated seat and started reading the book left for her.

"The Sinister Legend of Moth Murphy."

Chapter 14

The Sinister Legend of Moth Murphy

(Unknown, compiled from various interviews and unofficial stories, c. 1927)

Kenneth Jeremoth "Moth" Murphy was born in the now-defunct Poplar Valley, Georgia, the child of Irish immigrants Conchobar Liam "Conlee" Murphy (1829-1855?) and Siobhan Kelly (1831-1849). It is believed that he received his nickname both from his middle name and from his clothes being known for being full of holes, as if he himself was moth-eaten due to his family's poverty. Little is known about his mother before the trip to America, as she died giving birth to young Kenneth. He was raised by his father and later by his stepmother, Rose (1839-1868), who gave birth to his half-brother, Colm Peader "Peter" Murphy, in 1852.

For all of his father's hard-working spirit, he was not good at child-rearing and because of his long hours as a tradesman and lack of material goods, was frequently violent with young Kenneth. Conlee was known for being taken by the spirits, both in alcohol and in fervent emotion, and combined with his exposure to impurities in the nearby coal mines, he would have brought turmoil into his home.

From what we knew of the time and that area of Georgia where they lived, Kenneth may have even played near the mine, and exposure to all that toxic material may have led to the young Kenneth's own lack of impulse control and emotional instability in later years.

However, toward the end of his father's life, he worked fewer and fewer hours, which kept the chemicals away from his children, giving his youngest child a chance to be both physically and emotionally healthy.

It is believed that two major events led to young Ken's dark future. First, Conlee died when he was very young, which left him as the oldest male and primary breadwinner of his house at the age of six. He took on any work that he could, as a carpenter, a cobbler, a potter, wherever there was some money and the need for an apprentice. He took special skill and patience as a cooper, where he understood how wood reacts under pressure and the weather. He also became the sole protector of his younger brother, which became more and more difficult as they got older. Peter had a knack for finding himself in trouble, either from his curiosity leading him into streams or near cliffs, or by roaming into the wrong parts of town where wild animals still roamed or where Irish immigrants and their families were not welcome.

The second major event that affected Ken Murphy was the Civil War, where he saw the political push for an end to slavery and freedom for Blacks. His stepmother Rose was an avid reader and found it important to teach her children about the Missouri Compromise and the Kansas-Nebraska Act.

She had heard about the ransacking of plantations throughout the South, and of the carpetbaggers and scalawags that plotted to take away what little they had. Rose had taught both of her kids to be suspicious of "these people," of their "true nature" and of how they were looking to push them out of their new land, and even try to send them out of the country after they pillaged everything from their home.

Peter had rejected these ideas. He still ran off to areas in the outskirts of town and met different types of people who were passing through, including the Negroes that were looking for work and homes to build their lives. He saw the determination in their eyes to move on and remain peaceful, and he saw that his mother's words were dangerous. He left the home when he turned thirteen, eventually moving to North Carolina to become one of those scalawags that he heard so much about growing up. It was rumored that his descendants found their way back to the area around Poplar Valley, though that would not be until several generations later.

Ken Murphy, who was starting to be more formally known as "Moth," adopted his mother's ideas of the superiority of the white race. He began learning from prominent local white supremacists, including a local cooper named George Douglas. Moth went to work as an apprentice under Douglas, who recognized his talent, hard work, and dedicated focus in craftwork, as well as his impressionable mind.

Moth witnessed his first lynching at 17 years old. The mob caught a young Black male for allegedly stealing livestock and other supplies from a barn. The sheriff would have handled the issue in any normal circumstance, but the mob insisted on taking custody from the sheriff's deputy, who was powerless to stop the citizens exacting their own justice. Ironically, because the man was supposedly free and not considered property, there was no recourse for delivering him to a slave master. The community of white men, some of whom Moth knew personally and had done work for, brought this Black man to a large tree outside of a local bed and breakfast near the town of Lincoln and hung this man with little fanfare.

Moth was initially shocked but did not turn away. Rather, he saw the greatest expression of community he had ever seen, brought about by what he saw as the good, hard-working people of his community. For him, this was right. For him, this was justice. This was the way.

Two years after witnessing that first lynching, his mother Rose died of a terrible fever. Moth had felt such profound grief from watching his mother leave him. The grief was so painful that he refused to work, choosing instead to walk around his home and throughout the streets. He was inconsolable for weeks, drinking bathtub liquor and eating only minimal amounts of food to keep from passing out. He lost a lot of weight during this time and was rumored to have stayed slender with ashen skin for the remainder of his life. But it was during this time that he started his journey into becoming the infamous legend that he is today.

During his mourning period, he witnessed another lynching. The townspeople had accused a free Negro man of the murder of an unnamed man, theft of his property, and the rape of the now-deceased man's wife. He walked into the mob that gathered around the big tree in front of the local bed and breakfast to watch the town enact its violent justice. Moth slid through the group of men, and some women and children, to the inside of the lynching circle. He looked into the eyes of the young man, arms tied behind his back, standing on a small stool, filled with fear of what was to come and the resignation that he had no way to stop it. The man, somehow feeling Moth's gaze upon him, turned his head down to see him. Moth felt the intense stare, and something brilliant and menacing happened inside of him. Those that were nearby said that a heat came from Moth's skin, cutting through even Georgia's summer sun.

Moth was overcome with rage, fueled by grief, and driven by determination. He pushed aside a child standing near him, marched into the center of the circle, and kicked the stool without any warning, much to the shock of the lynch mob leaders. The Negro man dropped with a quick snap, but the fall did not instantly kill him. The man began to twitch in agony, trying to stare straight ahead with as much defiance as possible. Moth seemed to regret his decision, and he quickly picked the man up by his legs, as if to save him temporarily.

The crowd gasped in more shock and confusion, wondering why the child acted so outrageously only to pull away from the task at hand. The Negro man, for a brief period, felt relief from the child. Suddenly, Moth looked up with a twisted grin and let the man's legs go again. The man began to shake again, this time with less determination than his first drop. The surprise of being let go again made it difficult to maintain his stoic staring. The twitching became more erratic and his legs kicked back and forth more. Some were still surprised by what happened, while others began to smile as they saw their victim struggle more. Moth, not convinced that he had done enough to break the man's spirit, lifted his legs again then pulled his legs down quickly, causing more strain against the man's neck. The hanging man had suddenly realized that death was not coming soon enough, and he began to panic. His body was now shaking and tossing like a fish out of water. He tried all that he could to take his own life and end the pain, but he lost control of his body, trapped in his own panic. The crowd began to clap and cheer and carry on. Moth noticed that applause and that commotion, and he started to love it. He picked up the man's legs one more time and held him up to delay the torture even more, which made the crowd quiet down in anticipation.

Once he captured the crowd's attention, he brought down the man's legs one final time, rolling forward into a kneeling position after he completed the final pull. As the man shook in agony, Moth extended one leg out into a bent position, as if he were asking a young lady to marry him. He lifted his hands in the air with palms up and chest out, and he released a big, guttural shout to the crowd. At the same time, the man took his last, merciful breath. Moth did not allow this man to keep any dignity in death. The crowd cheered the man's broken spirit as bonus to their vengeance. The crowd loved what Moth did. The crown loved Moth. And he loved them.

Moth was fascinated by how he could handle the crowd. He had inspired the town of Poplar Valley and its brand of vigilante justice by inspiring showmanship, as if to bring the life of P.T.

Barnum himself into their routine of violence. He was also happy about the money that the crowd gave him after the lynching, for a job well done and for amusing them. Fortunately for him, the citizens of Poplar Valley were active in snatching various Negroes that came through the area, giving Moth and his followers a unique show for all to see. Soon, he was being asked to lead lynching proceedings, like a little drummer boy heading into battle. He traveled to neighboring towns to help them conduct their own shows, how to bring new gadgets or to take new poses for yourself or your unsuspecting victim.

His profile and his money were growing. He used some of the money to buy new items or build costumes. He had even convinced his partner George Douglas to assist him with support, giving young Moth extra income to come up with new ideas. George began to act as his manager, making sure that Moth's activities were listed in the newspaper or preparing his materials for easy access.

He coordinated how often Moth would come about new victims, because the public would become bored or restless, and Moth did not have enough time to create new themes without having a little space in between his events. He also started managing the money. While a large percentage of the payments were made using standard U.S. currency, George and Moth also accepted old Confederate money. They believed that the Confederacy would rise again to dominate the South and eventually the country, so they kept some Confederate dollars just in case.

Moth's neighbors and fans came to him with ideas for new types of rope, bindings, and other torture tools. He had learned new techniques for added pain, such as using different knots on the nooses that would delay the choking while he danced or told stories. He experimented with different types of fuel to set bodies on fire, particularly at night so that they would create a brilliant glow. Some of these fuels would explode like fireworks, with colors and shapes all around. He even modified some of his barrels with odd shapes to increase pain or include nails facing the inside so that the people he stuffed inside them would be pierced repeatedly while panicking to escape.

And Moth was not above killing any Negroes that he saw fit. For them, it was simply point and accuse. Most were men, but he was rarely given the chance to do the same to women.

He had been asked to go after two women throughout his life, but he did not follow through on either. One woman heard stories of him and recognized the description being passed around, so she managed to escape. The other was let go for unknown reasons.

On his rise to fame and fortune, he married Susanna Douglas, George Douglas's daughter. They had one child a few years later, Rosanna Siobhan Murphy. While Moth reveled in his lynching work, he tried to shield Rosanna away from the violence. Some felt that children may be a bit too young, although Moth was introduced to it at a young age and children had been known to attend Moth's lynching events all the time. Some who despised him felt that he knew what he was doing was wrong, though there was nothing that he publicly expressed to support this. Unfortunately for him, Susanna died shortly after

Rosanna found out about his work. She had come across her father hanging a man when she was twelve years old after her friends tricked her into seeing a lynching. She saw the swollen, mangled body hanging from the large tree outside of the local inn, then fell into shock and disgust watching her dad leading a crowd in howling cheers while sharing water jugs and baskets filled with food.

When Rosanna confronted her father, he did not provide an answer, only more drunken cheering, and incoherent ramblings about how important this was for securing her future and the future of Georgia. She was horrified at seeing who her father really was, and Rosanna took off running into the trees behind the inn. Moth decided not to run for her, as she would just tire herself out and come back to her father eventually. After several hours without his daughter returning, he went home to find his daughter gone and her things missing. Moth went out to gather his pack of loyalists to go into the woods to search for his daughter.

He brought at least twenty men from the community into the woods, tracking through every corner until nightfall. They went back for the next three nights. It was rumored that Moth had gone crazy, becoming more enraged almost every hour. They never found her, and she was presumed dead. Moth was never the same after the failed search. He thought that his daughter was the victim of revenge for his rampage through the Negro citizens of the town. Over the next several years, Moth became more erratic and sloppier in his work. His elaborate shows moved away from spectacle and more toward the grotesque, using more exotic instruments or desecrating the bodies beyond recognition. It was hard to watch, and fewer people began to appear over time, save his truly horrible followers, those that were grotesque themselves. With waning fans in Poplar Valley, Moth decided that his show needed to move from a few vagrants to hunting Negroes before they came into town.

He began leading his crew near the town of Lincoln, seven miles away from Poplar Valley, where new freemen established a city during Reconstruction. Moth's reign of terror was so well-known in Lincoln that a security system of citizens was established to protect each other, complete with firearms and escape plans if he were to appear. But even without considering Moth Murphy, Lincoln residents knew that the residents in Poplar Valley saw their existence as a threat, and even the kindest citizen of Poplar Valley was not keen on freemen living so close to them and could not be trusted to keep away from causing trouble. They also knew that they could not rely on the protection of the U.S. Marshal, the sheriff, or the courts.

The vast space between most towns would not allow officials to reach Lincoln in time, and Black Codes were still in place without any hope of reversing the laws. As a result, Lincoln was a hypervigilant town, and any potential danger that could come from Poplar Valley or any other town would be dealt with swiftly.

Moth knew not to go directly into Lincoln, lest he get himself or any of his crew killed. So, whenever they went there, they made sure to stay on the edges of the town, plotting and prodding for years. Usually, they would disrupt deliveries or scare away a postal worker whenever possible. Occasionally, they would abduct a Negro that would try and enter Lincoln, usually someone they knew was not from around the area. They figured that no one would care too much, and they would bring the person back to the inn in Poplar Valley and kill him. But after a few years, Moth became bold, and his followers became bolder.

One day when he was feeling emotional, Moth finally took his show into Lincoln proper. Someone spread the rumor that an unmarried Negro man was stealing livestock from Poplar Valley. Even though no one had reported their livestock being taken, Moth decided to march straight to Lincoln with his army, which had grown to at least forty men. Their information led them to a house near the edge of Lincoln next to a peaceful, babbling creek. The selection was good for them, as going to this house helped his team stay away from any real damage.

Moth walked up to the door of the house and knocked hard, yelling for the person to come out. He heard steps moving close to the door, and he saw a figure walk up to the door through a small slot. Without any hesitation, he kicked the door down in a single, swift kick.

The door flew off its hinges and fell on top of the person, pinning them to the ground. Moth walked right on top of the door with the pinned person underneath, drew his knife from his belt, and plunged the blade through the small slot of wood, pushing the blade into the person's chest. His men flooded into the house to look for any other people, screaming and howling like they were possessed by demons. The men went to the back of the house and found a man later identified as Jeremiah Brown. They dragged him out to the front of the house, beat him mercilessly, and strung him up on a tree branch. The entire episode happened within three minutes. Another group of men grabbed an infant child from a small tub in the bedroom, in the middle of a bath and playing with the water. Another group of men took the crying, naked child toward the creek, holding her in triumph over their heads as they continued their lust for blood.

Moth was confused. He thought he dealt with the man under the door. Who was under the door that he was standing on? He stepped off the door and lifted it up, only to find the mangled face and bruised body not of a Negro livestock thief, but that of his daughter Rosanna.

Stunned in horror, Moth picked up the door and looked at what he had done. Rosanna's left hand had been crushed under the doorknob. Her face, arms, and shoulder were covered in wooden shards and splinters. There were multiple pieces of wood pushing through her abdomen, and there was a large cut in her chest where Moth's blade sliced into her. Her eyes were swollen and rolled back. There was no sign of life. She was dead, and there was nothing that Moth could do to bring her back.

But before he had time to mourn, Moth stepped outside to see what his crew was doing and to try and stop the carnage from continuing. He realized that if Rosanna was staying with this man, then she took him as a husband. That means that more than likely, the baby that they took from the home was her child and, thus, his grandchild. With his daughter dead and no other family in his life, Moth went looking for the mob that snatched the baby. Unfortunately, the baby had been taken to the creek. Moth screamed for his team to stop, but the child had already been released into the air, her little bones hitting with a soft thud against the creek's rocks, watching slowly as the child's little body tumbled underneath the water and out of sight. Moth watched as the last of his known bloodline was killed at the hands of his own mob.

In retelling the story later, citizens of Lincoln noted that Rosanna had been found by a Negro youth in the woods shortly after her disappearance from Poplar Valley. Not knowing who she was, he took her back to his home for a meal and a place to sleep. She stayed longer than she had expected, in which time they fell in love. Residents of Lincoln knew that Jeremiah had taken her in, and while they knew what to look for with Moth Murphy, no one really knew what his daughter looked like, if they even knew he had a daughter at all. They could not get married, and no one in Georgia would have recognized their union, so they remained in hiding, raising their daughter Lilith, and taking on odd jobs and farming to make a living. Jeremiah Brown had always been kind, giving, and strong. Rosanna wanted only to get away from her old life. Both had wanted to see a better world for themselves and Lilith. None would live to see that world.

Moth was beside himself. He felt his malice and rage disappear, as well as his motivation to carry on. It was easy to be angry when he thought someone had snatched her away or murdered her. He can rally the gangs around him to take their sweet revenge against an endless number of Negroes that he felt wronged him. He had dealt with her loss the only way he knew how to deal with any big emotions – violence. But knowing that his daughter was alive and well until that moment, until she was killed by his hands, it broke him. He saw his daughter die for a second time that day. He crushed his daughter under that door, he plunged the knife in her to finish her off. He watched the last of his blood destroyed by the very mob he incited.

Without any thought, he went back to her body and tore a piece of her sleeve from her shirt, a thin piece of lace that did not require too much effort to pull and tied it around his wrist. He felt more and more numb, and after that day, the once youthful Moth Murphy began to deteriorate.

He began to lose the drive in his lynching shows. He passed the responsibilities to his much younger disciples, who, filled with the fire of youth, would treat them like mob attacks, conducting raids against Black farmers around Lincoln and travelers without even pretending like the person did anything wrong. Moth's barrel-making dropped in quality, causing his business to collapse. This was the most profitable business in all of Poplar Valley, with craftsmanship known throughout Georgia, so without his barrels to transport materials and sell to neighboring towns, the economy of Poplar Valley diminished. Moth was depressed and stopped eating, which caused him to wither even further than before.

Moth felt himself fade from existence and took desperate

measures. He had not been a religious man for many years, and he finally went to the local church to find forgiveness for what he had done and suffer penance for his actions. However, as the story went, the local minister had been away on the very day that he went to the church. That part of town had cleared out because of rumors of another mob coming for Poplar Valley.

He found two people at the church – the Negro owner of the local bed and breakfast on the outskirts of Poplar Valley and Lincoln, where he had seen and performed his killings without any retribution, and her daughter, who was always known for her puff of curly hair tied back by a bright orange bow. The family was known for being very spiritual and otherwise kept to themselves. They knew that protesting the lynch mob on their property would lead to certain death. Staying away helped them avoid the wrath of the lynch mob for so long. But with Moth Murphy's decline, the innkeeper was finally free to be herself. Moth had gone to the woman and begged her to help him find peace. She agreed to do it, but that the church was too central a place and could be a target, and that going back to her inn would be safer and would allow her to channel the spirits. Moth agreed and they went back.

They moved slowly behind buildings, to not be spotted by any remaining citizens of that part of town. After ten minutes, they came back to the bed and breakfast, where the owner told Moth to get on his knees below the large tree in front of her inn. She told her daughter to fetch her a wooden box near the register. Moth knelt beneath the majestic tree, which had been the site of his first lynching and where he had done the same many times before. He closed his eyes to ask for forgiveness and the hope that he would see his family in the future.

Just then, he felt a stinging pain in his back and a shock to his brain.

Falling over, he had not noticed the knife that the owner had plunged into his back, the one that she kept in the box to defend herself. Before he could get up to fight, she pulled the knife out and pushed it into his back once again, this time catching one of his lungs. She pulled the knife out a second time, using her foot to pull it out and simultaneously push him to the ground. The lady turned Moth onto his back and stared him down, all while her daughter watched. No one can be sure what she said to him as he lay on the ground dying, but there was one anonymous account of her last words to him.

"You will not receive forgiveness today, Moth Murphy. I know who you are, and I have seen what you have done. You have kept my family in terror for far too long, and you have allowed my home and place of business to bear witness to it. I was once in fear of you, fearful that you and those that follow you will take everything. Then I realized that without my own peace, you would have taken everything anyway. You are not forgiven until you pay your debts to the people of Lincoln and those that come after, to those whose lives you took for your own entertainment. To fill the void in your body. Life for life. Blood for blood. Until then, may you find no rest."

The owner had not seen the Lincoln citizens coming down the road from the direction of the lake to fight against the men of

Poplar Valley, nor did she see the men of the Valley coming up the road on their way to Lincoln. With both groups of men in her sights, she stuck the knife in Moth Murphy's body one last time, ending the terror of the Negro citizens.

The two mobs ran toward each other with vigor and ferocity. It was a bloodbath. No one was known to survive, and after the bodies were removed several days later, the citizens of both Lincoln and Poplar Valley moved away, never able to trust that the other would not come back to seek vengeance. Within two weeks, both towns were removed from all official maps. The inn that stood there fell into disarray until it was gone, presumably demolished, and the ground underneath the large tree remained red for decades from the blood that was shed that day.

No remains of Moth Murphy, the innkeeper, or her daughter were ever found, and no credible stories on their whereabouts exist.

Chapter 15

March 20, 2007, 7:36 PM

Aida stared at the last page. She was not sure what she had just read or from where this book came. It brought back the memories of that night, the trauma that she had felt so many years ago as a teenager. Was that Moth Murphy that she saw? How was that possible? Someone from the 1800s should not have been there, and yet, everything in this book represented something real she had seen before - the hangings, the burnings, the barrels, even the smaller details. And was that the same innkeeper and her daughter? How did she and her friends see them? Who was this woman that left her the book, and why did she dress like the little girl that she saw at the Cottonwood? Was the Cottonwood *that* place? Aida was overwhelmed with emotion, so she walked away from the table, went into a secluded research room, fell to her knees, and quietly wept.

She stayed in that room all night, crying until she fell asleep on the cold, thinly carpeted floor. The room was so isolated that not even the library volunteers had bothered to check for anyone until the library intern saw her early the next morning, still asleep on the floor.

"Dr. Barnett? Are you okay, Dr. Barnett?"

It was one of Aida's students who had stayed on campus during the break. He knocked vigorously on the window of the door, thinking that she was in distress.

Aida woke up slowly. Her student was looking through the window of the door with a deeply concerned look. She wiped crust from her eyes, dried tears from her cheeks, and opened the door.

"Huh? Alex? What are you doing here?" Aida was lightheaded from standing so quickly.

"Dr. Barnett, you're in the library. Do you need any help?"

"No, no, I should be okay." Aida wiped her face and adjusted her clothing. "I'm fine. I will see you in class in a couple of days."

"Um… okay, Dr. Barnett. I'll see you later." He walked away before Aida could close the door and exit the room.

Aida went back to the table where her belongings remained untouched. She gathered her things, grabbed the book that was given to her, and walked to the librarian's desk to check out the book. The librarian inspected the book.

"I'm sorry, Dr. Barnett, did you bring this book with you into the library?"

"No, I… found it in one of the collections."

"Well, that's funny. There's no tag on the book for me to scan, and there's no record of this book as part of any collection we have at the school."

"Oh, well then, what should I do?"

"Well, it's not one of ours, so I guess you're free to take it."

Aida was still confused but did not argue. "Okay, well should I bring it back when I'm done with it?"

"Dr. Barnett, there is no record, so as far as I'm concerned, the book is yours to do whatever you would like with it."

"Oh." She tucked the book into her bag. "Well, thank you. Have a good rest of the weekend."

"You too, Dr. Barnett." Aida hastily left.

Without much time to get back home, Aida went to her office to review emails and read through a research paper submitted to her by a graduate student before the spring break. After the quick office visit, she drove to the common area outside of city hall, stepped into the brisk spring air, and sat on a bench near a recycling bin. Aida pulled the mysterious book out of her handbag and read through the story again. She read it multiple times. As she read the account of this monster, Moth Murphy, she saw visions of her friends.

Each account of his methods looked remarkably like what

happened to her friends. The hanging, the burning, the barrels with the nails through them. She thought of his stringy hair and his pale skin and thought about what it could have looked like back then, with all of the terror that he brought with him. He was awful, and he inspired people for so long to do so much harm.

She looked around as she was thinking. She looked at the people coming and going from city hall. She watched children walking by and throwing coins into the old fountain. She saw bicyclists and runners and people on afternoon dates holding hands. She looked up and saw an old street sign that remained in place with streets that no longer exist, as an old memorial to what stood on the grounds before city hall was built. She looked at the steps going down to a small, constructed lake, with paddle boats for public use. She stared at the cobblestone border that lined the concrete walkways and fell into deep thought. Then, in a flash, she looked at the lake again. Then the memorial sign. It took her back to the memory of sitting with Lisa on a bench during her run at the lake. She remembers looking up at the sign near the bench – LEYLI. A hand-painted sign that had been there for as long as she could remember, with a history that had been forgotten for so long. She repeated the word to herself, annunciating each syllable a little harder each time. LEYLI. LEY-LI.

LEY-LI.

LEY-LI?

She read the book again. She went over the part about the two towns. Lincoln and Poplar Valley. Poplar Valley. Lincoln. She wrote the two words next to each other. POPLAR VALLEY LINCOLN. She stared at it. Then she saw it clear as day, right in the middle of the two town names. LEY LI. *Was this the historical sign with directions?* There were no arrows pointing in any direction and no markers denoting why that sign is even there.

For now, it was only speculation, but it was not the most pressing idea in her mind.

She was bothered beyond the story she was reading. For one thing, she never really saw anyone being killed. She found Luke hanging, and she found BG in the tree. The only person that she saw being killed was Marcus, and only because Edmond swung an axe into his chest in front of her. She was not even sure that Edmond had been alive before they found him near the barrel.

Was he alive? Did I actually kill him?

I was driving the car, and the barrel did bounce around a lot.

Was that the point, to make me do it?

Aida was sick to her stomach and doubled over with nausea and a headache. She decided that the rest of the day would be best spent at home. She packed her things into her bag and drove back to her apartment to take a nap, hoping to return to her thoughts when her head was clearer.

Fortunately, Aida did not have any lectures or office hours until the middle of the week when students returned to classes, so she was able to sit comfortably at home and think about what happened at the lake and how it tied to everything she read in the book. She remembered the man that fit the description of what Moth Murphy might have looked like, but there were no illustrations in the book, and she did not know if there were any photographs of the time that could help. She was not aware of where to begin with corroborating the story. The man she saw was in full black, and there was nothing in the record that could connect him to this person.

Then she remembered something – the lace. It was so out of place against his ashen skin and black clothing that she had almost forgotten that the man had a piece of lace around his wrist. Again, there were no pictures that could give her any insight, but was this the connection?

She thought about the young woman that she met at the library, the one that vanished into thin air. She remembered the orange ribbon in her hair and how it reminded her of the little girl that she saw at the Cottonwood. She could see the words that she read in the book. She remembered the stories that Esther told her before they left, about the boy who was hung on the big cottonwood tree. She read the account in the book and could see the words coming from her mouth. She could see the faces of her friends as they died in front of her.

Luke, hanging in the night sky. BG, set aflame on the ground. Marcus, an axe buried in his chest. Edmond, whom she imagined peppered with holes in his body and broken barrel pieces on the pavement. She saw Lisa running away to get the car, and Lisa again in anguish over learning about BG, the love of her life. In her mind, she saw Lisa's face as clear as the first day she met her in track and field practice, then the face fading away slowly, dissolving into darkness. Then, another thought came to Aida. The mysterious man flew past Lisa. He could have taken her first if he wanted to, especially if he had the strength to take BG so quickly and easily. But he moved right past her.

How could he have killed four people?

Rather, how was he able to get four people to kill themselves?

With Luke, no one saw him die, he was just found dead. With BG, he was still alive when they saw him, and letting him down started the fire. Granted, there was no way to know what was on him and the entire scene was designed to kill him. Marcus was killed by Edmond, but Marcus's last words were also strange.

He wasn't coming for me.

Marcus was never a target.

Then why was he running?

Moth Murphy could have taken Edmond too, but Edmond was taken only after he killed Marcus.

Was Edmond being punished for killing Marcus?

Luke and BG did not do anything to warrant their deaths. Then again, neither did Marcus. It felt like a setup.

She spent the next few years doing her own research. She dug deep into the archives, scrambling for any information that may lead to answers. She looked over old laws in Georgia, laws on citizen's arrests and government-sanctioned vigilantes. There were stories of mobs taking Black citizens out of police custody and lynching them on the spot, often by hanging. Men who were looking for work would be stolen from the streets and put into the court system, accused of bogus charges, or convicted of crimes that were not even crimes of our era – vagrancy for not being employed, looking in the wrong direction at the wrong person, attempting to vote, anything that "good-natured" people would see as a threat to their lives. But how did that tie to Moth Murphy?

Official records never mention him by name, save one obscure newspaper that she found recalling a man with a similar description – tall and ashen with long, dirty hair – and his proficiency of violence. The newspaper even mentioned how he revolutionized the use of his barrels, made in the same death trap that killed Edmond. And it was always the same, a young Black male randomly taken, with several allegations of random violence against Black towns that were defenseless against the white mobs.

How did this connect with Moth Murphy? How would a ghost have been able to do that? Was he something supernatural? Was it a copycat? If it were him, it would not have fit his style. He only killed Black people in Lincoln and travelers to the area, and from Aida's account, only one Black person died that night. Aida reread the account from the book. Luke and BG were white, and Edmond was Japanese. Then, she had another idea. If it was Esther in the book, then maybe he was paying the debt that Esther had given him. Was Moth Murphy somehow exacting revenge from beyond the grave? If this is true, he may have attacked not only other white people, but also anyone that had wronged any Black people? Maybe he was avenging the citizens of Lincoln? Maybe their descendants? That would explain everything that happened that night, but it was a far-fetched idea. She would have to believe that such a spirit had existed and caused terror for all of these years, and that the spirit was paying back a blood debt to an innkeeper and her daughter, the latter of whom grew up to leave her a book for her to learn this story.

She read through the materials several more times, and difficult as it was, wrote out what she remembered from so long ago. She conducted internet research to see if she could produce any other stories. There were several articles on websites dedicated to conspiracy theories and other fringe sources. For something so hard to believe, she had to move away from the official literature and go into the depths.

Some websites tracked the spontaneous deaths of several young men from the early 1890s through the late 1980s. All the victims were white males, roughly between the ages of 16 to 30. All had been found with some type of mutilation, and all within the same general area. Many sites posted maps showing where the victims were found, in the same general location as Poplar Valley. Every timeline ended at the death of her friends, and there were no logical explanations for why certain individuals died. Because of the deaths of Marcus and Edmond, there was no pattern, no unifying traits other than being male and of relatively youthful age.

She remembered the hate in that man's eyes. She saw that he was not above killing her. She knew that she was saved by the words that Marcus had spoken to her just before he died.

"He wasn't coming for me."

Marcus had mentioned that his family found their way back to the town after years of being away. Is his family descended from Lincoln? That would make some sense and fits with why Marcus would have been left alone, but that still did not explain everything.

Moth Murphy had willingly spared her life, and she needed to understand why.

Aida looked around her apartment, trying to process her feelings, trying to bring together what she figured out. She looked through her working papers and the stacks of books on her shelves and on her tables. She saw plastic take-out bags strewn about, hanging on shelves and under chairs. She saw the one bowl that she frequently used for eating, and the single fork that she used for her two-dollar noodles from the night before. Everything, both physically and emotionally, was a mess. She could not focus. There were too many outstanding questions, too many things that happened on that fateful night to see the whole story clearly. But beyond everything that happened, she remained. She was allowed to live. She was the only one to bear witness and tell the tale, made all the more confounding than when she started the research.

She was too tired and decided to get comfortable for the night. She changed into a loose white t-shirt and a pair of old Lorro High School sweatpants from her track days, which she could still fit into after so many years. The pants were draped over a chair, sitting next to a picture of herself and her three sisters at the beach. They were the famous Barnett sisters, all smiling and having a fun time, all with their beautiful golden hair and slim features. All except Aida of course, whose dark curls and tanner skin made her stand out against the rest of her family.

She stood up and looked at the picture and thought of more innocent times. She remembered that day fondly, with her and her sisters running along the beach, kicking sand in the air. She looked at her youngest sister Emily, smiling brightly, even though she was peeling from her sunburn. All of her sisters burned that summer, but not her. She lingered on that picture, looking at her paler sisters with their straight, dirty blonde hair, then back at her younger self with those dark curls and tan skin. Then she looked back at her sisters. Straight, dirty blonde hair, pale skin. Dark, curly hair and her tan skin. Dark, curly hair. Tan skin.

Something clicked in her head. She needed answers. She needed to see her mother. She needed to go home.

Chapter 16

June 16, 2007, 4:52 pm

Aida drove back to Lorro after so many years. She was fascinated by how the town had changed. Chain restaurants and department store outlets, which were not common when she was growing up, had moved into the city. The open areas where Aida spent her days laying the in the grass and running around with her friends were restructured into large, enclosed pavilions with metal benches that were conveniently spaced to take a break when walking while being just uncomfortable enough to discourage excessive dawdling and encourage shopping. Streets were expanded from narrow two-lane town roads to larger four-lane thruways, and several acres of space were claimed for bigger parking lots.

The Lorro Mall looked like it was sliced apart and swallowed by several big-box warehouses and national chain restaurants, an earth-colored maze with human rats bouncing from storefront to storefront. Surely, there was a group of real estate developers and construction moguls waiting for more human rats to fill the gaps.

Aida drove around unfamiliar faces and figures strewn across clean white brick stones and fresh black asphalt roads. People were walking toy breed dogs and wearing clothes inside out. She found her way around the new parks and drove through Forrest Estates, where Luke and Marcus's families used to live. She thought about them and choked up. She continued past the Estates on her way to her mother's house.

A small discount store existed where the Nakamura's general store used to be. The Nakamura family left Lorro after their son died, and little was known about what happened to them. Most people speculated that they moved back to Japan, some believed that they moved north, but all were certain that they would never return. Their store used to be near a very distinctive tree that shined with purple and pink flowers when spring was in full bloom. Neither the store nor the tree was there anymore.

BG's family was still in Lorro. People rarely saw them, even their own neighbors, though they had never been particularly social to begin with. BG was a nice person, but other than dating Lisa, no one had a strong feeling about him one way or the other. His death was sad, but unfortunately not celebrated in the same fashion.

This helped his family in one way. Much of the intrigue around the killings centered on Luke and Marcus, the two kids from rich families, and this helped BG's family grieve in peace. His parents did not want to answer any more questions about the story or their feelings. After their mourning period, his mother went back to working in

Lorro city hall, and his father went back to his job as a clerk to a local municipal judge. They continued to serve in their official capacity to the citizens of Lorro, unwavering in their work to the people. Their colleagues supported them quietly, and they avoided any further scrutiny.

Both Luke's and Marcus's families stayed in Lorro for as long as they could. Both of their families had long, deep ties to the area and supported each other through so much heartache. The home association at Forrest Estates provided the funds to hold the funerals for not only their families, but also another smaller joint service for all of the families of the victims. The joint memorial service was held in the downtown square, where the new mall stood today, and with the exception of Lisa and her family, the entire town attended. Luke's family eventually moved to Eugene, Oregon, where they could feel more at ease and start a new life. Marcus's parents saw their daughter graduate high school, and the family eventually moved to the New York City area where she attended college.

Aida went to the memorial gravesite for her friends before she went to her mother's house. The memorial stood prominently against a few gravestones peppered throughout the church's field. Until recently, the town was not heavily populated, so there was plenty of space to move around. The memorial tomb was a large stone tree atop a dull grey block with a reddish tint, adorned by small stone angels and old flower petals shriveled against brown, crusty stems. She looked at the names etched into the old block.

Lucas Ian Murphy
Marcus Garvey Dixon
Brandon Garrett Thomas
Edmond Nakamura

She allowed only a few tears to drop. She did not want to breathe life into that memory or give any more power to the past, so she did everything to bottle her emotions. It looked like the names were ordered by which family donated the most to the stone. She knew some of the families would be petty about things like that. For them, it was always a competition. She left her competitive spirit in the past, along with the rest of her troubled memories. She knew that it was futile.

Four dead classmates. Four dead friends. Four human stories gone from the Earth, and all that remained was this stone and some wilted flowers. Aida had nothing to leave for them. The most valuable thing that Aida ever had were the memories at the lake and the love that she had with them before everything happened, and she wanted to forget even those things for good. She stayed for several minutes to say her final goodbye, then turned her back on the stone, walked back to her car, and drove away.

Aida reached her mother's driveway a few minutes later.

The reddish colors of the sunset blended against the reds and browns of her mother's roof and the dull yellow of the exterior walls. Aida's mother was sitting in an old rocking chair and staring deeply into the distance. She was not staring at anything in particular. Rather, it was as if she were watching her own life story from a distance and did not want to disturb the show. Aida slowly exited her car. She did not want to ruin her mother's concentration.

She gently walked up the porch steps. Her mother looked up to see her looming over her like a dark shadow, the light from the sunset radiating from behind her like an angel coming from above. She leaned up from her chair and opened her arms for a hug. Aida hugged her back without any hesitation.

"I'm so happy to see you, dear." She winced slightly while she leaned back into her chair. She showed the signs of her aging.

"I'm happy to see you too, Mom."

"How long has it been, dear?"

"It's been a little while."

"Oh, Aida, I think it's been a little while longer than a little while."

Aida gave a nervous smirk. "Yes, I suppose."

"Come sit with me." Aida's mother pointed to a small stool across from her.

"You look thirsty. Let me get you something to drink first."

"That would be lovely, dear. A nice glass of lemonade for the both of us. It should be on the counter."

Aida entered the house and looked around on the way to the kitchen. Not much had changed. The old family pictures from before were still hanging along the walls. She saw one of the last pictures that her father had been in, showing his wrinkled skin and the constant glimmer in his eye that never faded, even as he became sick. Over the fireplace mantle were some newer pictures of her older sister Dana with her newborn baby. There was one picture with the baby not smiling, but all the other pictures of the baby included Aida's mother, grinning and hugging her tightly.

She found the large pitcher of ice-cold lemonade beading with condensation that left a puddle of water on the kitchen counter. She grabbed two glasses from the cabinet next to the refrigerator and poured lemonade halfway in each glass. She opened the fridge door and took out a bottle of iced tea, which her mother always kept in the house, and poured a small amount into one of the glasses. Her mother had always enjoyed her lemonade this way.

Aida came back to the porch and gave her mother the cold drink, then pulled the stool next to her mother and sat down with her own drink. Her mother was staring straight out to the world again.

"How are you feeling, Mom?"

"Oh, I get better every day. Can't really complain." Her mother did not break her stare.

"That's really nice. And you're taking your medication?" Aida's mother had developed diabetes in her later life, so she was taking metformin pills regularly.

"Yes, dear. Twice a day, just like the doctor ordered. Your sisters are always calling me to remind me. It's a little irritating." She took out a pill from her medicine bottle and tossed it into her mouth. She chased the pill with the iced tea and lemonade mix, then started biting into a half-eaten banana that was laying on her lap. She finished eating in silence.

"How have things been around here? It looks like things have changed a lot."

"Yeah, it's been an adjustment. A bunch of big-box stores moved in and drove a bunch of the small guys out. Once we saw the Nakamuras closing up shop, we knew it was over." Aida's mother took a big gulp from her drink. Aida's eyes welled up. "That family, they were good people. They took a lot of crap from some folks around here, and to be honest, there weren't enough people sticking up for them, myself included. But between losing their kid and losing customers, I'm surprised they stayed around as long as they did."

"When did they leave?"

"I think they stuck around till about 1997, so about ten years after you left high school."

"Do you know where they went?"

Aida's mother took another big gulp and rested her hand on her lap. "Nope. They just took off. I hope they're okay."

"Well if you want, I can try and find them online. Maybe send them a DM."

"Send them a what?"

"A DM. A direct message."

"Is that different from an email?"

"Yeah, you do it through a different site?"

"Can you just email them? Isn't email direct enough?"

Aida shook her head and chuckled. "Mom, don't worry, I can find them."

They sat for a few seconds, taking deep breaths, and staring into the sunset. Then Aida's mother remembered something and chimed in.

"Hey, did you ever catch up with that other girl? Lisa was her name?"

"Yes, I sent her a DM." Her mother turned to her and grimaced. Aida smirked at her mom.

"How's she holding up? Her family took a lot of crap, too."

"Last time I messaged with her, she was doing fine." She welled up again, this time shedding a couple of tears. "I found her just to check in because it had been so long. She said she had family in Maryland that took her in until they found a more permanent place to stay.

She kept running competitively, even through college, and started picking up lacrosse too. She said that she doesn't get out that much anymore, except to compete. But she did say that she married a German guy that she met in Gothenburg during a world competition."

"That's good that she got someone from outside the U.S. so she wouldn't have to deal with all the stuff you guys went through."

"Well, that's the interesting part. He knew about the story?"

Aida's mother was perplexed. "How?"

"Mom, it was a pretty big story, and with the Internet, there's not much you won't find out about."

"And what happened? He didn't think she had something to do with it, did he?

"Nope. He read the story, and he didn't care. He just loved her, and they got married."

"That's really sweet, I'm happy for her."

"Me too. I asked if she wanted to keep in touch or get together the next time we were in each other's cities."

"Are you gonna do it?"

"She never responded to that message. So, probably not." Aida and her mother both took sips from their drinks.

Aida's mother waited several seconds before continuing. "And how have you been feeling these days?"

Aida hesitated briefly. "Oh, things are the same. It gets a little better with me, too. I just keep with my research and move forward. As long as I'm focused on my work, things are great. Hopefully, I can get published in something major."

"Have you gotten back into running at all?"

"Nothing competitive. I haven't done anything like that in a long time. Only some light jogging to try and stay in shape. No more marathons or anything like that. I don't really push myself the way that I used to." She paused briefly and looked away. "I...I don't really have the heart for it anymore."

Her mother frowned and sounded contemplative. "It's a shame. I wish I could have helped you more. I didn't know what to do. Maybe if I just didn't let you..."

"Mom, please," Aida responded. "I don't want to go back over that. I've been through enough." She hesitated again. "Also, that's not why I'm here."

"Oh? So you didn't just come to see an old woman sit?" Her mother gave a smirk and a small chuckle.

Aida smiled slightly, showing no teeth. "Well, not really. I actually wanted to ask a couple of things about our family."

"Like what, dear?"

Aida quickly gathered her courage and just blurted it out. "Did our family own slaves?"

Her mother turned to her slowly with an incredulous look, followed by a very open and hearty laugh.

"Ha! Is that a trick question?"

"Or maybe they did something foul in the past? Like they were crooked?"

Aida's mother sucked her teeth. "Honey, our family didn't even get to this country until well after all that had ended. We didn't own slaves. Hell, until about a few years before I was born, our family didn't own much of anything."

She kept laughing.

"Yeah, that's what I figured." Aida laughed slightly, only to remain comfortable with her mother. "It's just that, something tells me that I'm different. And I don't mean, like, our family's different. I mean, that I am different, even from everyone else in this family. I know it doesn't make much sense, but something feels off."

Aida's mother did not stop staring, but she sat up straight. She wanted to hear more. "Tell me more about this… feeling."

"Well, I see old pictures of me and my sisters, and I don't feel like I belong. I was never really into anything that they liked, and sometimes they would give me these weird looks like I didn't belong in the house. I mean, I love them, and I know they love me, but it didn't always feel like things were exactly the same." Aida pulled her speech back and curled forward. "I don't know, it's just weird." She did not tell her mom about what Moth Murphy did that day.

Her mother sighed, leaned back in her chair, and went back to staring away. "Oh, Aida, you're too smart. I could keep lying to you, but I'd rather not anymore. You've always been so sharp, and I've gotten so old."

"What do you mean?"

"I mean, you're right. I don't know how you figured it out, but you're right. You are different."

Aida became anxious. "How am I different, Mom?"

"Well, there was a time that your father and I weren't doing so well. Remember I kept telling you that our family didn't have anything? We *really* didn't have anything. Hell, until about a few years before your older sister was born, our family didn't even own much of anything. We didn't have the house, and our money situation wasn't in the best shape. At one point, we were just going to call it quits and leave each other. I would have taken your older sister and moved up north to be with your grandma and grandpa in New York. But then, your two younger sisters wouldn't have been born."

"So what does that have to do with me? You wouldn't have had me?" Aida felt a lump in her throat. She trembled in anticipation.

"You? Well, here's the thing. You probably would have still been born... with or without your father in the picture."

Aida became more flustered, her heart racing at learning

the truth. "So you're saying… that my dad isn't my dad."

"No, I'm not saying that. Your father was always your father. He always took care of you. He loved you, and he provided for you and for this whole family. And I never told him anything else about what happened. He told me that if we worked things out, he'd love you all the same, even before you were born. I guess that's what kept us together, his sense of duty and our love for each other and for you girls."

Aida's mother gave a heavy sigh as she had another sip of her lemonade. "But you are another man's child. I never told him who it was. He never asked questions. And if by some chance he knew, he never told me about it."

Aida relaxed her body and sat limp over the stool. She was trying to process what she was hearing. Somewhere deep down, she knew this was what her mother was hiding from her, and after the initial shock, she finally had some relief. They sat there for a few minutes, drinking their drinks. Aida became more calm. Her mother continued to stare into the distance.

Finally, Aida broke the silence. "So, are you going to tell me who it was? Was it some random person that you met at a bar somewhere two towns over?"

"Oh, nothing like that. Aida, you already know the man."

Aida became stunned again. "But you never told me

anything about it before."

"Yes, I know. What I'm saying is, you've always known the man that was your father. Your biological father, I mean. I'm not sure if he even knew you were his daughter. I'm sure he had his suspicions, as well."

Her mother paused to take a sip of her cold drink. Before Aida could even ask the question, her mother casually answered it for her.

"Aida, do you remember Marcus Dixon's father?"

www.ingramcontent.com/pod-product-compliance
Ingram Content Group UK Ltd.
Pitfield, Milton Keynes, MK11 3LW, UK
UKHW041955190726
13854UKWH00005B/1976

9 798986 302218